ROMY SOMMER

By day I dress in cargo pants and boots for my not-so-glamorous job of making movies. But at night I come home to my two little Princesses, and we dress up in tiaras and pink tulle … and I get to write Happy Ever Afters. Since I believe every girl is a princess, and every princess deserves a happy ending, what could be more perfect?

Follow me on Twitter @romy_s.

Also by Romy Sommer

The Trouble with Mojitos
To Catch a Star
Not a Fairy Tale

Waking up in Vegas

ROMY SOMMER

HarperImpulse an imprint of
HarperCollins*Publishers* Ltd
77–85 Fulham Palace Road
Hammersmith, London W6 8JB

www.harpercollins.co.uk

A Paperback Original 2014

First published in Great Britain in ebook format by HarperImpulse 2013

A catalogue record for this book is
available from the British Library

ISBN: 978-0-00-755977-0

Automatically produced by Atomik ePublisher from Easypress

To my parents for their love and support, and to Rachel and Imogen for putting up with all those hours I spend on the computer.

Chapter One

I wish I were dead. Phoenix moaned and pulled the pillow over her head to block out the blinding light and the clamour of rain. If only her head would just explode and get it over with.

At least the pillow seemed softer this morning. And it smelled nicer than normal too. A fresh citrus scent that quickened her blood.

Hang on a minute. Rain? In Vegas?

She peeked out from under the pillow. *Oh my…*

Not her room.

This room was at least twice the size of her entire motel apartment, and way better furnished. Correction: this wasn't just a room; it was a palatial hotel suite. Through the double doors she spied a living room.

She sank back on the pillows, which seemed to be dusted in gold glitter. Perhaps she'd already died and this was heaven. Though she highly doubted heaven would want Phoenix Montgomery. Not that she'd been a particularly bad girl, but she'd never made much effort to be particularly good either.

And she'd certainly seen and done a few things a more conventional person might quail at. This being one of them.

1

She covered her eyes. Blocking the sunlight streaming in through tall windows at least helped the ache in her head.

Sunlight? Then that wasn't rain…

Instantly awake, she turned her head and identified the source of the sound of running water: not rain, but a shower running.

She wasn't alone.

Terror clutching her heart, she lifted the crisply starched sheet. *Oh hell…*

Beneath the sheet, she was stark naked, aside from yet more gold glitter. And not alone, in a room she didn't recognize.

What the hell had happened last night?

Through the aching blur, she fumbled for memories. She and Khara had got off work not long before dawn, and they'd gone out for a drink as they often did at the end of a shift. They'd chosen a pool hall away from The Strip, the kind of place that wasn't in any tourist brochure. With the sedatives the doctor had prescribed to help her sleep, Phoenix hadn't had that much to drink. Besides, she could handle alcohol. Unless…

There was only one thing that could get her drunk.

She closed her eyes, grasping for the memories. They'd danced to music from an old-fashioned juke box and played a couple of games of pool. She'd even won a little money off a guy with tattooed arms who couldn't believe he'd been bested by a girl.

And then there'd been a man who bought her a drink…

The bathroom door opened. Phoenix sucked in a breath and opened her eyes.

Yeah, that man.

God, but he was drool worthy. Especially wearing nothing but a fluffy white towel wrapped around his hips. He definitely worked out. Until now she'd believed six packs like that were the results of air brushing in magazine spreads. This set of abs was one hundred percent real.

She forced her gaze higher, over the tanned chest, broad shoulders, up to meet a pair of startling blue eyes in a face framed by overlong fair hair.

"You're awake. Good. I've ordered breakfast."

She was so not hanging around for breakfast. She cleared her throat. "Where are my clothes?"

He pointed toward the living room. Clothes lay strewn across the floor and, yep, there it was, the only thing that could get her truly and embarrassingly drunk… a bottle of champagne, empty and lying on its side on the floor.

"How are you feeling?" The demi-god's voice matched his face; deep, masculine, with a hint of amusement and a faint Germanic trace.

He perched on the edge of the bed. He smelled as good as he looked, clean and slightly lemony. Just like the pillow. Her blood all rushed south again.

She could only imagine how much fun he'd been up close and personal. Pity she had absolutely no memory of it.

"Did we really…?" She waved a hand at the bed, and her naked body beneath the sheet that she now held clutched to her breasts. And her heart stopped.

Was that a ring on her finger? On her left hand?

She clutched her head in her hands and groaned. "Please tell me we didn't…"

She shook her head. Sex with a virtual stranger was one thing, but there was no way she'd done the M word.

He laughed a low, throaty chuckle. "Yes, of course we did. It's going to take some getting used to, isn't it? Who'd have thought we'd meet our destiny in Las Vegas?"

Destiny? He had to be kidding, right? There must be hidden cameras in the room. If this was someone's idea of a joke, it wasn't funny. Whoever the pranksters were, they'd better be paying her a lot of money. She rubbed her temples. "I need coffee."

"I've ordered coffee and fresh orange juice with breakfast, but you should drink the juice first." A knock sounded on the distant door to the suite. "Great timing."

As soon as he turned his back to let the room service waiter in, Phoenix made a mad dash for the bathroom. One look in the mirror was all she could bear. While Demi-God had that tousled, fresh-out-of-bed-and-can't-wait-to-get-back-in-it look, she just looked as if she'd fallen asleep drunk.

She bolted for the door and rubbed her throbbing temples. *Think, think.* What the hell had she done? And more importantly, what the hell was she going to do now?

Steeling herself, she turned and checked her reflection in the mirror. Glitter? Seriously? She was so not a sparkly, gold glitter kind of girl.

First things first. Shower. Clothes. And then she was getting the hell out of here.

She turned on the shower as hot as she could bear and stepped under the stream. Then she leaned her forehead against the cool, tiled wall. *Okay memory, you can come back now.*

The ring on her finger was bigger than a wedding ring, a masculine thing, more signet ring than wedding ring. A pattern of stylised roses wove around a blue stone carved in the shape of a dragon's head. She was no jewellery expert, but she guessed it was made of silver and lapis lazuli, and was very, very old. It was the kind of ring one used when one married on the spur of the moment without any planning.

Not the big, flashy diamond ring the producers would no doubt supply if this were an episode of *Pranked*.

She groaned aloud. She couldn't possibly have agreed to get married last night, even on a bad mix of sedatives and champagne. Though Demi-God sincerely seemed to think they had.

Demi-God also needed a name. She thumped her head against the tiles, but that didn't help. One memory sprang to mind, though. They'd gone dancing in some swanky nightclub. And boy, could he dance. A sudden clear image surfaced, of his hands on her waist as they slow-danced, locked in their own little bubble on a dance floor, surrounded by grinding, gyrating bodies.

Desire flashed through her, so strong her knees threatened to buckle. If that was her reaction when he wasn't even in the room, could she perhaps really have done it? Could she have married him in an endorphin-fuelled high?

She used his lemon-scented body wash and scrubbed her hair with the masculinely-branded shampoo. Feeling at least a little better, she switched off the water and stepped out the shower. The towels felt even fluffier and softer than they looked. Whoever Demi-God was, he could afford one of the best hotels in town that was for sure.

Whether he'd won it all in the casino last night, or earned it the regular way, she didn't care. Either way, she hoped she hadn't signed a pre-nup.

She shook her head. *Focus, Phoenix.*

She needed clothes, but hers were strewn across the floor of the suite, and getting to them would mean having to face Demi-God again. She wasn't ready for that.

Beside the door hung a cotton bathrobe. This was Vegas. As long as she wasn't running down the street naked, she could probably still hail a cab without getting arrested for indecency. She covered herself and faced the mirror again. Much better.

Now she had to figure out an escape route, preferably one that didn't involve having to get past her new husband first. Morning After small talk was bad enough without having to throw in '*Who the hell are you?*' too. Not to mention, heaven only knew what her endorphins might do if she had to face him again.

The window.

There was only one, high up over the massive spa bath. She climbed up on the bath ledge and wrestled with the latch. With an ominous and over-loud squeak it finally gave way, and she shoved it open as far as it would go.

Damn. Regulation four inches.

"Are you okay in there?" Demi-God's voice sounded very close to the bathroom door and her heart hammered.

"I'm fine." Insane, crazy, desperate, but just fine.

Phoenix looked back at the window. It was high. It was extremely narrow. But as long as she didn't breathe, she could do this. She hoped. Arms, head or legs first?

She'd only done this once before, but if she could do it once, she could do it again. All she needed was a ledge to stand on once she was out and a drainpipe to shimmy down. This time should be even easier, since she was barefoot.

As there was no curtain rail to hoist herself up with, she opted for arms first. Squeezing her eyes shut, she gripped the window frame, and pulled herself up. Then carrying her weight on her arms, she leaned through the gap to look out. And wished she hadn't.

No frickin' way. She wasn't afraid of heights, but this was high. And this certainly wasn't anything like that three storey boutique hotel in Miami she'd escaped from. Even if she could squeeze herself through a four inch gap, there was nothing but a thirty storey fall on the other side. Give or take a few storeys.

Four inches was a whole lot smaller than she remembered. Her arms were scraped by the time she managed to wriggle backwards onto solid ground.

Okay, re-group.

She sat on the cold toilet seat and wiped her arms down with a damp facecloth.

One bonus. At least now she knew it was morning. Probably

tomorrow morning. Which meant she hadn't just lost a few hours, but had a whole day and night to account for. And at least one bottle of champagne.

Well, she couldn't change what was past, so she would focus on the here and now. Since escape wasn't an option, she should unbolt the door and go out there, get her clothes, tell Demi-God '*That was fun. Have a nice life*' and leave the traditional way.

Or she could sit right here until the maids came in to make up the room and use them as cover to duck out?

Option B it was. She stuck her hands between her knees. Had the bathroom shrunk? The walls seemed to be pressing in.

"You still in there?" The voice on the other side of the door sounded concerned now.

"Sure. Where else would I be?" Spread across the asphalt thirty storeys down?

"The coffee's getting cold."

At the thought of coffee, her mouth watered.

"You want to talk?"

No, she didn't want to talk. She twisted the ring around her finger. The craftsmanship was certainly awe-inspiring. The carved silver roses even had petals. Nope, the producers of *Pranked* definitely weren't that imaginative.

"I hope you're not having second thoughts this morning." This time Demi-God didn't sound at all concerned. He sounded amused, confident no woman wouldn't want to be married to him.

I've got news for you.

"I know it's sudden, but see this as just another fun adventure," he said.

Sure. Like root canal was fun.

"You know I thought I'd be the one needing time to adjust to the idea. Are you sure you're okay in there? Is there anything I can get you?"

7

He wasn't going to let her be, was he? If she didn't go out there and face the music, he'd probably call Security to bang the door down. Actually, that could work...

But if she had to sit still another moment longer, she'd go mental. "I'm fine. I like my coffee black, one sugar."

When she heard the clatter of coffee cups in the distance, her stomach growled. Maybe staying for coffee wouldn't be so bad. She could explain this was all a big mistake, get dressed and leave like any rational person. She could do rational.

But if she was going to do this, she wanted a rough idea of who her host was, where she was, and how to get home.

She rummaged through the bathroom cupboard. There was nothing there except the usual hotel branded toiletries. At least now she knew where she was. The Mandarin Oriental.

Talk about getting lucky. She'd always wanted to spend a night at the Mandarin.

Next, she tackled the leather toiletry bag beside the sink. Jackpot!

A small container of headache tablets with the name Max Waldburg and the contact details of a pharmacy in Napa.

Mrs. Waldburg ... no, that definitely didn't sound like her. Hell, Mrs. Anything didn't sound like her. She was a tumbleweed, an adventurer, not a married woman tied to some man she barely knew.

She swallowed one of the tablets, combed her hair, then found a complementary airline toothbrush and toothpaste in the bag, and brushed her teeth.

Okay, she was as ready as she was ever going to be. Sucking in a deep breath, she headed for the door.

The first thing to assault her senses as she emerged from the bathroom was the scent of bacon. Her stomach flipped in ecstasy. She was starved. Maybe coffee and bacon, and then she'd get away.

The suite was decorated in a slick Asian design, in soft creams and browns, but what grabbed her attention was the panoramic cityscape beyond the floor to ceiling windows. It looked a whole lot better from this angle, when you weren't dangling over the drop.

Max sprawled on the sofa, reading a newspaper. He grinned up at her, a dimple appearing in his cheek. "Ready to eat?" He waved at the dining table that had been set for two. Including polished silver cutlery and a crystal vase full of yellow roses.

He set aside the newspaper and moved to join her at the table. "The flowers are for you, to make up for the ones you didn't have at our wedding yesterday."

Did he know they were her favourites? She shook her head. She didn't want to know how much he knew about her from yesterday. And she hadn't even been able to remember his name. Guilt and shame crowded her, but she pushed them aside. Life was too short for regrets.

And with her stomach doing some serious complaining, life was also too short to reject a good meal, no matter how awkward the circumstances. Who knew when she was ever going to afford to eat at the Mandarin again?

Pulling on her metaphoric big girl pants, she sat across from Max at the table and spread the real linen napkin across her lap. No paper napkins here.

And the bacon was every bit as good as it smelled. Like a good girl, she drank the glass of orange juice Max handed her. He was right about one thing; she felt a whole lot better with the food and juice inside her. It certainly beat her usual bowl of cereal, eaten standing up in her elbow-room-only kitchenette. And the view was way better, without looking at what lay beyond the windows. Wasn't it just her luck that she pulled the most gorgeous man she'd ever met, and she couldn't remember any of it?

When they were done, Max cleared away the plates and poured the coffee. Fresh, full-roasted coffee with cream. Phoenix couldn't help but lick her lips in anticipation.

Max rocked his chair back as he sipped his coffee. "So what shall we do today?"

"I need to get to work." Or anywhere but here. Besides, if this was really tomorrow, then she was supposed to switch to the day shift today.

"No, you don't. Khara offered to take your shift today, remember? After all, we're on honeymoon."

Khara was in on this? Phoenix was going to wring her neck as soon as she got back to work. Friends weren't supposed to let friends drive drunk. Or get married while drunk, either.

She swigged down a mouthful of fortifying caffeine. "Well now, that's kind of the problem. I don't remember."

Max's forehead furrowed. "What don't you remember?"

"Everything. Anything. The last thing I remember was you offering to buy me a drink in the pool hall."

She wished she had a camera for the expression on his face. *Floored* didn't even begin to cover it.

Then a smile crinkled the edges of his eyes. He obviously smiled often, because the crinkles deepened so naturally. "I guess I'll have to remind you, then."

With a grace she could only hope to emulate, he rocked his chair forward and grasped her seat with both hands, yanking her closer.

He wasn't even touching her, yet his proximity sent a rush of static heat through her. And when he slid a rough hand up her thigh, parting the robe … now she understood why she'd married him. Endorphin city. The sex must have been the best of her life. She damned well hoped her memory returned soon, because there wasn't going to be a repeat performance anytime soon.

She pushed his hand away and clamped the front of her robe closed. Clamped her knees shut too, but that was more to ward off the sudden wave of desire shooting through her. He had her wet and needy and all he'd done was touch her leg.

She shifted her chair away from him, far enough away that she could breathe again, and reached for her coffee cup. "So tell me about yourself."

His brow furrowed again. "You seriously don't remember anything from last night?"

She shook her head.

He blew out his breath, grinned and stuck out his hand. "Hi, my name is Max. It's a pleasure to meet you Miss…?"

"*Ms.* Montgomery." She couldn't help but smile back. He had that kind of infectious grin that was really hard to resist. "But you can call me Phoenix."

"Interesting name. Is it your real name or a nickname?"

"I'm not telling. At least not until we've dated at least six months." And none of her relationships ever lasted that long.

"Okay. But if you prefer, I can always call you Georgiana."

She flushed all the way down to the roots of her hair. How much had she told this complete stranger yesterday? She never told anyone her real name. "Since I'm obviously at the disadvantage here, I don't suppose we could speed this up a little? Like full name, place of birth, age, job description?" *The reason why I married a complete stranger?*

He eyed her for a long moment and she resisted the urge to squirm. For a mad second she thought he was weighing something up and deciding how much to tell her. God, she hoped he wasn't a con man. That would be awkward if she was left with the bill for this fancy suite. She didn't think her life savings would stretch to breakfast, let alone a night in this hotel.

Then he smiled, mouth wide, eyes crinkling, and her heart thundered against her chest. With a smile like that, it was amazing he was still single. Well, single enough to marry her, of course.

Assuming he wasn't some Mormon with three wives back home.

Was bigamy legal here in Nevada?

"Max Waldburg. I was born in a tiny principality in Europe you won't have heard of, my age is on our marriage contract, and I work for my grandfather on his farm."

Farm. Napa. Something clicked. "A vineyard. You make wine."

"I'm a vintner, yes. Five years of studying viticulture, and a whole lot more as an apprentice to my grandfather, and the critics say I'm getting quite good at it."

He reached for her hand, and this time she didn't push him away. His touch was more than a caress; it was as if she stood in a rainbow, in a shaft of sunlight on a cold day.

"You'll love it there. The farmhouse has a wrap-around veranda and a kitchen the size of forever. You can stand at the front door and look out over the entire valley and see nothing but vines and trees. At sunset, it's truly magical."

She'd married a poet. That figured. She always managed to attract men with very little grasp on reality. "You were born in Europe, but your family's American?"

"My mother's family is American. My father was from Europe, but he's dead now. He died a few weeks ago."

"I'm sorry. My father died recently too." And this was the first time she'd thought of him all morning. She'd been awake nearly an hour and not once had the familiar grief overwhelmed her. Max might have his uses after all.

He squeezed her hand. "I know. That's what drew us together in the first place."

She didn't need to ask what drew them together in the *second* place. The delicious static buzzing between them spoke for itself. And if she didn't put a little space between them very quickly, she was going to find out first-hand how good the sex had been. She wasn't usually a girl who slept with a guy she didn't know. At least, not when she was sober.

She pulled her hand out of his and slid off the chair, away from him. Pacing the floor was preferable to being seduced by the deepest, darkest blue eyes she'd ever seen.

Blonde hair, blue eyes, tanned skin. He would make a good surfer boy if he ever decided to give up farming.

"So we signed a marriage contract?"

He laughed. "It's on the side table. Knock yourself out." The idiom sounded quaint in his subtle accent. She took advantage of his offer and leapt at the envelope on the small table he indicated. The papers inside seemed genuine. And that really was her signature, messy beside his large, looping, slightly old-fashioned scrawl.

"Is there a pre-nup?"

"We won't need one." His confidence bordered on arrogance. "There hasn't been a divorce in my family in over three hundred years."

She had news for him. She could only track back two generations of her family, and there hadn't been a divorce in any of them that she knew of either. But that didn't mean there couldn't be a first time.

On the plus side, her impetuous little marriage could be her ticket out of a dingy motel in Vegas. Max had wealth and privilege written all over him. "So what's your big plan for our future?"

He leaned back in his chair, lips curling in a smile. Did anything bother him? Did he ever stop smiling?

"We'll go back to Napa, of course. And we'll make wine, and enjoy the sunshine, and clean air and good food. We'll have a family, and we'll grow old together."

Phoenix was ready to stick her finger down her throat. Stay in one place the rest of her life and grow old there? Stay with one man, forsaking all others? Over her dead body.

She dealt with the easiest issue first. "Why do I have to uproot myself and move to Napa? You could move here."

"Because I have responsibilities in Napa, to my grandfather, to everyone who works on the farm. You don't. Last night you told me Napa was as good a place to live as any."

She rolled her eyes. "I was obviously out of my mind last night. I *like* not being responsible for anyone or anything." Or *to* anyone. As long as she showed up for work every day and didn't spill drinks on the customers as they threw their life savings into the slot machines, her life was her own, to do with as she pleased.

Max leaned back. "That's a rather selfish way to live, don't you think?"

"Of course it's selfish. And I'm perfectly happy with that, thank you very much. So how do we go about getting a divorce?"

That wiped the smile off his face pretty quick. "I just told you there hasn't been a divorce in my family for over three hundred years."

"Then you'd better start making plans to have me bumped off, because there is no way in hell I'm going to settle down and play happy families with you. If the choice is between life as a soccer mom driving an SUV in the suburbs, and death, then it's a very easy choice."

"Who says it has to be either?" He laughed, and her tolerance level jumped from mild irritation to flat out anger.

She waved the papers in her hand. "This marriage is a mistake. Commitment is the quickest way to end a good relationship, and we don't even have that." Not to mention that it committed you to only one person, and where was the fun in that? No more waking up in strange hotel rooms and trying to climb out through windows? Thanks, but she'd skip it.

He frowned. "You don't really believe that."

"You don't have a clue what I believe."

"Last night we talked about having dreams. About a shared life together. I'd never met anyone before who wanted the same things I did until I met you."

"Last night was last night, but this morning you're dealing with *me*."

His voice was low and soft. "You're still the same woman you were last night, Phoenix."

She shook her head, refusing to listen. Bad move. The headache still pressing at her temples thumped harder against her skull with the movement. "I know I have a tendency to be impulsive, but I don't go around marrying strange men, and marriage is definitely not something on my Bucket List."

Max pushed himself up off his chair. "No, what's on your bucket list is to see the world. As soon as the harvest is in, we can do that. Together. Starting in Europe, as we discussed last night."

Okay, so she'd pretty much told him everything. Parents dead, check. Dreams and ambitions, check. Real name, check.

Even Khara, who she'd worked with – and partied with – for nearly two months didn't know more about her than her favourite music and movies. And she considered Khara one of the best friends she'd had in years.

Phoenix needed something stronger than coffee to deal with this. But since it couldn't be more than…she glanced out the window…ten in the morning, she'd have to settle for the sofa and resting her fevered head in her hands.

Even if she could magically grow wings and fly out of this suite, she'd have to stay. There was no way she could run away from this. Not until there were signed divorce papers next those marriage papers.

Max came to sit beside her on the sofa, but he didn't touch her. "Can I get you anything for your headache? Do you want to go back to bed?"

"Yes." One form of escape was as good as another. Then as that infernal smile tugged at his lips, she added: "alone."

Why waste such nice sheets and pillows? She could have a nap, and when the headache was gone they could have a rational conversation about getting divorced. And if she was going to sleep, it might as well be here in luxury, rather than in the motel where she could hear the couple next door bickering through the walls all day and all night. They'd lived there going on six years now. That was the thing with couples. They tended to get stuck in a rut, in a dead end. She wasn't ever going to get caught in a rut. She wasn't planning on staying in either the dead-end motel, the dead-end job or even this dead-end city, for more than a few months.

Besides, she'd come here for the memories, a final adieu to her parents before setting off alone into the wide world. But her parents weren't here. Vegas had changed since they'd lived here. *She'd* changed.

There was never any point in going back, only moving forward.

She struggled up from the sofa, but Max was quicker. He caught her up in his arms and, ignoring her protest, carried her back to the bedroom. "Second time I get to carry you across the threshold." His voice was low and husky, right by her ear.

"Please tell me we didn't follow every cheesy wedding custom? If we were married at a drive-through or by Elvis, I think I might throw up."

"Pink Cadillac, Elvis in a white suit, and everything."

She must have turned green, because he laughed, a deep rumble against her chest. "That was a joke. Except for the glitter guns, it was classy and intimate. And very, very private."

"I don't suppose you have pictures?" Not that she planned to keep a scrapbook of the occasion, but maybe they'd trigger a memory…

"No pictures." He smiled, and this time she had the distinct impression he was smiling at some secret. Almost gloating.

She narrowed her eyes. There was something she was missing

16

here.

"Shall I tell you a bedtime story?" An odd way to divert her, but she nodded. No-one had told her a bedtime story since she was ten and her mother died. Since Dad almost always worked nights, she'd usually been tucked away to sleep in some dingy dressing room, or in the corner of a brightly-lit green room. Dad always said it was her greatest accomplishment: the ability to sleep anywhere at any time.

His death had robbed her of that gift. Sleep eluded her most nights now.

Max laid her down on the bed and pulled the covers over her, tucking her in. It was certainly nice to be taken care of, and made for a pleasant change. And maybe, if she was really lucky, she'd wake up and find this was all nothing more than a strange dream.

She closed her eyes and didn't open them when Max climbed onto the bed next to her. He stayed above the covers but looped an arm across her hip. The weight of it was strangely comforting, in spite of the flutter in her heartbeat that accompanied it.

"A long time ago, in a kingdom far away," Max began. "There was a king who lived in a big stone castle. Since his kingdom controlled access to the river, he was a very rich and powerful king. Like all kings of that time, he married a wealthy princess from another land. It was, of course, an arranged marriage, and the king never bothered to make any effort to know his bride, or to love her. Instead he flaunted his mistress for the entire kingdom to see, giving his bastard children great honours, and carving up the kingdom between them. His subjects grew to hate him, and they hated his mistress even more, and when he announced that he was divorcing his rightful queen to marry his mistress, the people revolted. They appealed to the queen's family who sent an army, and for many years the little kingdom was torn apart by civil war.

"When the war finally ended, the kingdom was never again as

17

prosperous as it had been. The new king who took the throne, after his uncle was brutally and publicly executed, made a vow to his people: never again would any member of the royal family divorce. They would love their spouses and live quietly without scandal for as long as the kingdom remained.

"A powerful sorceress witnessed his vow and cast a spell on his family, a blessing on their marriages. Ever since, every marriage in the royal family has been a happy one, and the couples have always found true love with the one they married."

It was a very strange bedtime story. She'd never heard anything like it. But his voice was hypnotic, and his hand stroking down her hip was soothing. Phoenix sank back into sleep, the deepest sleep she'd had in months without the aid of sedatives.

Max lay beside Phoenix and watched her sleep. Awake, she had a vibrancy about her that made it hard to see the real woman behind the façade, but asleep the fragility beneath the surface was more apparent. Her slender face, with high, pronounced cheekbones and pointed chin, looked almost elfin.

After the restlessness driving him these last couple of weeks and the jet lag from all the travelling he'd done, it was an unexpected joy to do nothing. And to do nothing with the woman who turned him inside out every time he looked at her.

He hadn't truly believed all those stories he'd been raised on about falling in love at first sight until the moment it happened to him. It had been that way for his parents, and his grandparents, but he hadn't given his own marriage much thought.

But the moment he'd walked into that dive of a bar and seen Phoenix leaning over the pool table, concentration focussed on lining up her next shot, he'd been a believer. 'Moth to a flame' and all those other clichés had nothing on the instant attraction he'd felt for her. And it wasn't all due to the sexy, slender figure wrapped in tight jeans. Her appeal had been more than physical. She'd laughed as she'd lifted her head and caught his eye, and he'd been dazzled.

He still felt dazzled.

And she still hadn't removed his ring from her finger.

He stroked his finger lightly down her cheek, and Phoenix stirred in her sleep, full, pink lips curving in a brief smile as she sank deeper into sleep. She smiled a lot when she was awake, but that smile was nothing like this one. She seemed to have a public smile, a wide, bright one, and this smile, her more intimate, sexier one. Fitting. He knew all about the difference between the public persona and the private one, and it would make life easier on his wife if she did too.

He fluffed the pillow beneath his head and rolled on his back to look up at the ceiling. For the first time since he'd received the tearful midnight phone call from his mother, he felt at peace.

The big state funeral in the gothic cathedral in Neustadt had been more than he could bear. All that ritual and pomp for someone who was no longer there to appreciate it. It was life that should be celebrated, not death. So he'd said the right words, shaken the right hands, and got on the first plane back to the States.

He'd stood in the vast concourse at JFK and watched the flight announcements flashing on the large screens, and for a moment he'd wondered what life was really all about. He'd felt as if he stood at a crossroads, between a life only half lived and all those things he still wanted to do. Then the Las Vegas flight had shown up and he'd known that's where he wanted to be.

Destiny had called and here he was.

He traced a finger over Phoenix's lips. She'd met death up close and personal too. And she too had chosen to celebrate being alive. He'd never met a woman so full of life and energy, so dedicated to making the most of every moment, that in the space of an hour she'd made him feel more alive than he ever had before. It had taken even less time than that to lose his heart to her.

He had no intention of letting her go now that he'd found her. All he had to do was talk her out of this nonsense about a divorce.

Chapter Two

By the time she finally woke, Max had dressed, phoned his grandfather to check all was well at the vineyard, and glanced through the evening papers. He breathed a sigh of relief to see Westerwald's grief hadn't made the US press. The death of an unknown European Archduke was already old news and Max's anonymity was still safe.

Phoenix padded into the living room, rubbing her eyes, blonde, sun-streaked hair rumpled. Her hair was darker underneath, he noticed, and curlier where the strands touched her collar bone.

"What time is it?"

He folded the paper and set it aside. "Lunchtime. Shall we go out?"

"I'd rather not." She began to collect her clothes that still lay scattered across the floor, a vivid reminder of the passion that had overtaken them the night before.

"Perfect. I'm sure we can find a way to make staying in very pleasurable."

"I meant I'd rather not spend the afternoon with you."

He'd known exactly what she meant, but he wasn't having it. "You don't perhaps want to spend a few waking hours with me to find out why you liked me enough to marry me?"

She bit her lip, sorely tempted but not yet giving in. He could only imagine how galling it was to have lost a huge chunk of time. Possibly even more galling than having the woman of your dreams not remember you. Worse, not remember falling in love with you.

He wasn't used to either situation. He'd left Westerwald and made a new life in the States precisely because women had a terrible habit of falling in love with him. The trail of broken hearts he'd left behind had embarrassed his father's staid ministers.

Westerwald didn't handle embarrassment well. They preferred their royals dutiful and dull, and Max had never had an inclination to be much of either.

The States had been kinder to him. No-one here had expected him to be anyone but himself and no-one expected him to fall in love at first sight. Least of all himself.

He poured all his infamous charm into a smile. "At least give me this afternoon. I'll even pay. Sky's the limit. If there was anything you ever wanted to do in Las Vegas, this is your chance."

Phoenix clutched her clothes to her chest. "One afternoon but I get to choose how we spend it?" She paused, looking down at the slender fingers fisted around her clothes. "Deal. But you'll need to take this back."

She slid the ring off her finger and handed it to him, careful not to touch him. Max took the ring, keeping his victory smile to himself. An afternoon was all he'd need to remind her of what was so special between them. He'd have his ring back on her finger soon enough. And this time it would be a proper ring, with the most elegant diamond he could find.

This wasn't exactly the quality, getting-to-know-you afternoon he'd had in mind. Max pressed his foot down on the gas as the vehicle beneath him skidded sideways on the soft sand. He yanked at the steering wheel, only just missing the makeshift barrier by inches. There was no time for relief, though, as he hurtled towards the next corner. Phoenix's dune buggy was already two car lengths ahead, with the chequered flag visible in the distance.

He put his foot flat on the pedal but it wasn't enough. Phoenix's buggy careened over the finishing line a few yards ahead of his.

When he climbed out the vehicle, adrenaline still pumping, heart racing, and swept Phoenix off her feet, she laughed and wrapped her arms around his neck.

Her heart hammered against his chest, her full, round breasts pressed against him. Her pupils were wide and black as sin, swallowing the softer chocolate brown of her irises. She swallowed nervously, but didn't push him away.

His lips met hers in a crushing, possessive kiss, no less urgent on her part than on his. She tasted of excitement and passion, and he responded by pouring everything of himself into that kiss.

When they finally broke apart, she ran light fingers through his hair. "Now if you drove the way you kissed, you might have beaten me."

"Oh?" he asked, reluctantly letting her slide from his grasp to stand on her own feet. But he kept an arm loosely around her waist. It was good to have her back in his arms again, where she belonged.

"All or nothing. As if you had nothing to lose."

"Don't you have anything to lose?"

"Nothing."

Nothing to lose and no responsibility. There'd been times in his life he'd have given anything not to feel responsible for other people. But there was a flip side to being responsible. "But then you have nothing to live for either," he pointed out.

She shrugged. "Tell me you didn't feel alive sliding down that hill at a hundred miles an hour." Her face glowed with exhilaration, but he was sure her feverish flush had more to do with the kiss than the dune buggy race.

"Where did you learn to drive like that?"

"I had an ex-boyfriend who raced motorbikes. He bought me my first bike and taught me how to ride."

He forced his jaw to unclench. The afternoon was too short to spoil with talk of the other men in her life. And of course there had been other men in her life, and he better just get used to that idea. "So what's next? The zip-line in Fremont Street or the Stratosphere bungee?"

Though he'd rather not do either. Right now he'd much rather take his bride back to his hotel room and make love to her.

"Been there, done that. I need a shower." She shook her head to prove the point, scattering sand. They were both dusty and sweaty from the race.

"Fantastic idea." He still had his arm wrapped around her waist. He slid his hand further down, to hook in her jeans pocket. From her sudden, sharp intake of breath he knew she hadn't found the intimacy of his touch undesirable. Quite the contrary.

The first time he kissed her yesterday, they'd stood exactly like this. Admittedly, they'd both been cleaner then. And less sober.

Dragging in a shaky breath, Phoenix swatted his hand away and pulled out of his embrace. "Separate showers." She sent him a glare frosty enough to scare a normal man. "And no champagne."

Max forced a laugh and grudgingly stepped away. "Suit yourself."

So they headed back to his hotel and showered. Separately.

He was waiting when she emerged from the bathroom, fresher and sparklier than before, with all traces of both the strenuous afternoon and last night's revels gone, and for a moment he was sure her memory had returned. She was back in the bathrobe, the pale rounds of her breasts visible where the fabric gaped, and his blood pounded at the sight. But when he touched her, caressing her bare collarbone, she stepped out of reach, eyes distinctly cool.

What wasn't cool was the flush that blossomed where his fingers had touched her skin. She couldn't deny the chemistry between them, nor would she be able to avoid it much longer.

"Where are my clothes?" She eyed the now empty armchair where she'd discarded her jeans and T-shirt.

"Housekeeping have taken them for cleaning. You had half the desert in them."

"I hope you don't think you're going to keep me hostage here with nothing to wear but this bathrobe?"

He shook his head. "I got you something a little more suitable. You're not going to need jeans or a bathrobe where we're going tonight."

Without a word, she followed his gaze to the living room where a small mountain of branded boxes stood ready and waiting.

"I wasn't sure of your size, so I asked them to send up a range."

Her jaw dropped open. "What exactly do you have planned for this evening?"

Aside from the obvious? "For a start, dinner at Le Cirque."

Her eyes widened. "I've always wanted to eat at Le Cirque."

He only just stopped himself in time from saying 'I know'. She didn't like that he remembered so much while she remembered nothing.

Yesterday, in that blissful, whirlwind day they'd spent getting to know each other, she'd told him how frugally she lived, scraping together every spare cent for her trip around Europe. Money was the only thing she lacked, and Max wasn't above awing her with it to keep her at his side until she succumbed to the passion burning between them.

Max placed his hand on Phoenix's lower back as they threaded between the tables, enjoying the soft sway of her movement

25

beneath his hand. He must remember to thank the lovely lady at the concierge desk for her superb taste. The wrap-around silk dress in a delicate shade of teal moulded to Phoenix's curves like a second skin. It was classy and sexy at the same time, and he was having a problem keeping his hands off her.

The famous restaurant, with its decorated walls and swathes of bright-coloured fabric overhead, was surprisingly intimate and elegant for a room decorated to resemble the inside of a circus tent. The maître d' seated them at one of the most sought-after tables, at a picture window overlooking the Bellagio's famous fountains. Lyrical piano music underscored the muted sounds of conversation. Max held out her chair for her, before taking his own seat across the table.

While Phoenix studied the menu, Max chatted to the sommelier, finally ordering a bottle of wine from his own vineyard. In the time it took for the wine to arrive, he entertained Phoenix with a history of the wine they'd be drinking. Her eyes didn't glaze over, and she asked intelligent questions, so he figured she wasn't faking being interested.

"You love what you do," she observed, smiling and softening towards him as she first breathed in the aroma of the wine, then took a cautious sip. "Nice. Though I have to admit I know absolutely nothing about wine except how to drink it."

"Then you'll be my most honest critic." Her honesty was one of the most appealing things about her. He swirled the wine around in his glass. "Last night you told me you moved to Vegas because you lived here as a child. Tell me about it."

"I'm the one at the disadvantage here. You already know so much about me. Tell me about yourself."

He shook his head. "I'll get my turn." He wanted her to talk about herself, to relax and open up. In his experience, most people felt more comfortable talking than listening. He'd been trained to be a very good listener.

Phoenix didn't look at him but focussed her eyes instead on the view beyond the expansive windows. "The year we lived here was the happiest time I remember. Not that I wasn't happy a lot in my childhood, but my mother was still alive then. She sang in a show at one of the big hotels. She had the most beautiful bluesy voice imaginable."

Her mother, he remembered, had died less than a year after they'd left Vegas. Phoenix had been only ten. He couldn't imagine losing his mother. He'd been so lucky, surrounded by adoring parents, his beloved grandmother, nannies, and a brother who'd been in equal measure his best friend and greatest rival.

"My father had a day job playing piano in a classy restaurant much like this one," she continued. "We had dinner together as a family every night, and then Mom would read me a bedtime story, tuck me into bed, and go out to work."

"Sounds nice."

"Most of the time." Her restless fingers played with the stem of the wine glass. "But like everything in life, it didn't last. Daddy hated it – playing piano for people who barely heard it. As with all true artists, he needed to be challenged, to try new things. So he joined a rock band, Mom left the show, and we followed him on tour. After that, I don't remember spending more than six months in any one place."

"Must have been tough getting a decent education when you kept moving."

She shrugged again. "I got the best education anyone could ask for. I'm a graduate of the University of Life." She smiled that wide smile that lit up her face and made her eyes sparkle. There were gold specks in her dark eyes, he noticed, that gave her a luminous quality. "There's probably not much I haven't seen or done. And I read a lot. You can find out everything you need to know from books."

He didn't disagree. But her education was a world away from his. He thought of the six years he'd spent in an elite French boarding school, tied to a desk where books had been dry and dull, and life beyond the windows had seemed to pass him by. He'd dreamed of a life like hers.

He'd been destined for Oxford and the kind of studies that would turn him into a good diplomat, an asset to his country. A *dull* asset to his country. Until he'd bucked the system and chosen to study wine-making in California instead. His father had hit the roof and their relationship had never been the same since. Never would be, now his father was dead.

"What are you thinking about?" Phoenix asked. She laid a hand on his, and the heat radiating from her was both electric and calming at the same time, like being burrowed in bed beneath a warm duvet during a storm.

"I think we should order our meal. Have you chosen yet what you want?"

She frowned and released his hand.

Once he'd summoned the waiter, and they'd placed their orders, Phoenix turned her direct gaze on him.

He tensed. He'd told her a lot about himself yesterday. Now in the clear light of day, or at any rate the clear light of the sunset deepening over the desert, he was sure those confidences were better kept in the dark. He didn't want to freak her out until she knew him better.

"Tell me about your family," she prompted.

He sucked in a breath. This was the question he most hated. From the moment he'd been old enough to talk he'd been cautioned not to talk about family. One never knew what would make its way to the ears of the press. Which was why last night he'd chosen the most discreet chapel they could find in Vegas and why he'd used his fake ID.

But today Phoenix didn't have a clue who he really was. She saw him as nothing more than what he'd become, a Californian vintner. There was a freedom in that.

He sipped his wine, taking a moment to think through what he would say, how to skirt the truth without lying. He valued honesty above all else, and didn't want to start their married life with lies. "My father inherited the family business. He's always been big on duty and family."

"Was his death sudden or expected?" Phoenix cupped her chin in her hand, listening avidly.

"Very sudden. He had high blood pressure for years, but this was his first heart attack and he was dead within half an hour."

Sympathy filled her eyes. She nodded. "How are you holding up?"

No-one but Grandfather had asked him that before now. Back home in Westerwald the only thing everyone had been concerned with was "what now?"

He'd told the old man he wasn't sure. He still wasn't. "We were never that close. Rik was always our father's favourite son, the one most like him."

"That doesn't answer my question." Her gaze sharpened. She wasn't going to let him get away with the evasion.

"Conflicted. I feel guilty that I didn't make amends before he died. And of course I'll miss him. He was a big presence in my life, even if we never saw eye to eye."

"I sense a 'but' in there."

He sucked in a deep breath. "But now that he's gone, I feel as if I'm finally free of his expectations. Rik will take over the family business and I'm free to do what I want."

"How does your brother feel having to take over the business while you get to do whatever you want?"

He shrugged. "Rik has always been big on duty and family too. He's perfect for the job."

"And what is it you want to do with all this freedom?"

This was how they'd talked last night. She hadn't been afraid to ask him the hard questions. The deja-vu was both surreal and reassuring. The same connection they'd had last night was still there. She understood him. She listened. It hadn't been a mirage.

"I want to live life on my own terms, doing what I want, going wherever I want, when I want." He took her hand, entwining his fingers through hers. "And with whomever I want."

She caught the emphasis on his final word, and bit her lip. But she didn't pull her hand away.

"And I want to make good wine. There's a tremendous amount of satisfaction in making something that brings joy to others, even if it is only for a fleeting moment in time. Yesterday you told me that's exactly how your father felt about being a musician."

She nodded.

"And you told me you want to live life on your own terms too." He grinned. "In those exact words."

"I do." She blushed as her words echoed between them. She shook her head. "But my terms don't include marriage and children and mortgages."

He laughed. "I can promise you won't ever have to worry about a mortgage with me. And I'm in no hurry for children."

"Tell me about your brother." She was changing the subject, putting him off. That was fine by him. They had plenty of time to talk about starting a family of their own.

"Rik and I have always been close, though I guess we're like dark and light. He's the serious, thoughtful, dutiful one, and I'm the easy-going, push-the-boundaries one."

She nodded again, expression thoughtful. "I never had any siblings. I'm always curious how other people manage to share their parents. I'm glad I never had to."

"We never needed to share either. Rik was always our father's child, and I was our mother's. She had a higher tolerance level."

"Were you that naughty? No, don't answer that, of course you were." She laughed, a husky, sensual sound. "But what are you doing here now? Shouldn't you be with your family?"

He shrugged. "I'm here for the same reason you are. To have a party and celebrate the fact that it feels good to be alive."

Amusement lit her eyes. "And you thought getting hitched was a great way to celebrate being alive?"

"I didn't expect to meet my one true love here in Vegas, but now it's happened, everything's changed. I'd rather be here with you than anywhere else in the world."

Her eyes narrowed. "You're insane, you know that? You don't surely believe in true love and fairy tales, and all that nonsense?"

"Why not? Don't you feel this connection between us?"

"What I feel for you isn't a connection. It's lust. Pure and simple."

Pure and simple. Exactly the words he would have chosen for the state of his feelings for this wild, complicated, beautiful woman. But it wasn't merely lust he was feeling. He was well acquainted with lust, and this was a whole lot more.

But if that was all she would admit to, he could work with that.

The waiter appeared at her elbow, sliding their plates onto the table. When he attempted to refill Phoenix's wine glass, she put her hand over it. "No more for me." She sent the waiter a smile that had the poor man near melting.

"Is there anything else I can get you, ma'am?"

"No, thank you."

Alone again, her smile dropped as she turned back to him. "So did your parents fall in love at first sight and live happily ever after then?"

Max smiled, warmed by the memory of a family story he'd

heard over and over. "Pretty much. It started as a business merger of sorts. She was a model, stunningly beautiful, and my father's… board…decided she would bring a glamour and freshness to the company image. But from the moment they met, that was it. Destiny stepped in. By the time they married, they were very much in love, and haven't spent a night apart since."

"This must be a tough time for her then. So you plan to drop in on her while she's still in mourning and say 'Hi Mom, this is my wife. I know you haven't met her yet, but wey-hey it was love at first sight.'?"

"I hadn't thought that far ahead," he admitted. "I tend to just go with the flow in life." He stared at the reflections in the surface of the golden wine. "But I don't want to keep this from her for too long – we don't have secrets in our family. But you're right, now probably wouldn't be the best time to break the news. We'll leave my family out of it for a while. But you'll meet my Grandfather when we go back to Napa."

"I am not going anywhere with you. Except to find a lawyer to help us do whatever we need to do to erase the past twenty four hours."

She was certainly tenacious, he'd give her that. But if wine-making had taught him anything, it was patience. "Eat up. We have tickets for the show tonight."

"What show?"

"Cirque du Soleil, of course."

Her eyes narrowed. "I couldn't keep my mouth shut last night, could I?"

"Is it so bad that I know so much about you, your dreams and desires, and want to make them happen? All you have to do is sit back and enjoy the ride."

She clamped her mouth shut and focused on her food but her demeanour still screamed defiance. Max could hardly blame her.

If it was him with no memory of their marriage, he'd probably also balk at the thought of being trapped. No matter how gilded the cage.

Only for him this didn't feel like being trapped. It felt like coming home. It felt inevitable.

So he humoured her mood. He had no doubt she'd thaw when she had some time to absorb last night's events or remember them, whichever came first.

By the time their chocolate soufflé and coffees arrived, she'd warmed enough to question him about his studies and about the vineyard. These were easy questions, readily answered without too much thought, and when they were done and he'd paid the bill, she even let him take her hand as they walked out the hotel.

It was rather nice to walk hand in hand with a man who made her heart beat as fast as any adrenaline rush. They circled the vast plaza in front of the Bellagio Hotel and paused to look at the hundreds of fountains dancing in the waning light. A light breeze lifted the spray off the fountains and drifted it across to where they stood. The fine mist brought welcome relief from the heavy evening heat.

The sky overhead was the colour of blood, full of the drama and passion that only the desert could produce, a million specks of dust reflecting the sun's dying light.

For a mad moment she closed her eyes and wondered what it would be like, to let herself fall dizzyingly in love with someone, to give in to the passion.

She'd believed she was in love with life. But a sneaky feeling had started to creep up on her today, perhaps even since last night, that she hadn't really been alive until she'd met Max. She'd done crazy things before, tried every adrenaline rush she could find, and loved the thrill of being on the very edge of terror, yet somehow simply being with someone who warmed her from the inside out, was a whole different kind of rush.

It wasn't as if she hadn't been in lust before. This was … different.

Max stood behind her, one arm wrapped loosely around her waist, and she couldn't tear herself out of his embrace. She leaned against the railing, watching the water catch the setting sunlight in a million rainbows. She sighed. It felt too damned nice to be held.

Clearly it had felt pretty nice yesterday too for her to have done the unthinkable and married Max. What had possessed her? If only she could remember…

"What are you thinking?" he whispered in her ear.

"I wish I could bottle and sell moments like these. Soon it'll be dark, and the magic will be gone." She shivered. Nothing ever lasted. Nothing stayed the same. Change was the only constant. Relocation, death, amnesia.

The only way to cope when the things you loved were gone was to not let yourself feel. And with Max, she was very much in danger of letting herself feel.

She shook herself. "Let's get going. I don't want to miss the show."

She wasn't surprised to find their seats were the best in the house. Max did nothing by halves, it seemed. Since her first job in Vegas had been scalping tickets, she had a pretty good idea how much they'd set him back. Most people booked months in advance, and he'd made one phone call and got the very best.

If there was one thing she'd learned about Max today, it was that his wealth hadn't come as a recent windfall. He had that casual attitude towards money that marked him as born with the proverbial silver spoon in his mouth.

Clearly there was a lot of money in wine. The kind of serious money that could easily buy a ticket to Europe and a couple of months' worth of beer and pizza.

But at what price to her soul? She couldn't do that to him. Being shackled in marriage was bad enough. Being used was a step too far. She wouldn't do that to anyone, and especially not to Max, who had an honourable streak a mile wide, even if he had some very old-fashioned ideas.

After the show, they wandered through the Bellagio's very own indoor botanical garden, and then sampled cocktails on a poolside deck, in one of those private cabanas that Phoenix had only ever seen in brochures. She stuck to rum-based cocktails. They were way safer than champagne.

Max quizzed her on where she lived and laughed at her behind-the-scenes stories from rock concerts she'd attended. He wasn't like the famous or rich people she'd met, and she'd met more than a few in the nomadic life she'd shared with her father. Rock stars, record producers, even an A-list actor or two when they'd lived in LA. And she'd been spectacularly unimpressed by them all.

Max was different. He wore his wealth like a comfortable skin. There was no bling about him, just a certain expectation that he would always have the best. She'd love to see him in her drab little apartment in the far from fashionable suburbs. She couldn't even imagine it.

He carried himself with that air of assurance that he could have anything he wanted. And tonight he made it very clear he wanted her. The fact that for five whole minutes she allowed herself to contemplate giving him exactly that was a measure of how good he was at getting exactly what he wanted.

They strolled down Fremont Street, wandering among the pushing crowds beneath the neon signs, bombarded by voices, the heavy thump of music and the scent of fast foods.

Max held her hand and it felt like a life-line. Since her father's death she'd felt adrift, rootless but somehow in Max's company, laughing with him, talking with him, she felt anchored and safe.

It was very tempting to give in. What could it hurt? Just one more night. She'd already done the worst anyone could possibly do on a first date by marrying the man. Surely one night couldn't do any more damage?

So when they magically found themselves outside the Mandarin Oriental all the reasons she'd kept him at bay through the day seemed very hard to remember.

She pulled her hand out of Max's and faced him. It was definitely easier to think without his touch accelerating her heartbeat and muddying her thinking.

"I should get home," she said. It was a half-hearted attempt. She forced herself to sound more certain. "And I need a good night's sleep before I go to work tomorrow... because I know for a fact Khara didn't volunteer to take that shift too." The daytime tips weren't as good as the night shift, and Khara was working to put herself through college.

Max slid his hands down her arms, from shoulder to elbow, and she shivered in spite of the intense June heat.

"Are you sure you don't want to stay?"

No, she wasn't sure. She was far more used to giving in to her impulses than denying them. But look at the mess she'd made already - she was married to a man she barely knew. Hell, she was married. That was enough.

"I'm on the day shift tomorrow, so I get off at six. We could meet then if you want. I'll need to collect my clothes from you, and we should talk about filing papers."

His eyes narrowed, but his voice stayed level. "As you wish."

He dropped his hands from her arms, and it was as though a chill breeze suddenly swept between them. He summoned one of the hovering cabs.

"This has been a truly magical day," she said. "Thank you."

"It doesn't have to end, Phoenix."

"Of course it does. There's no such thing as magic. Today has been like a dream, but every dream ends when we wake up."

"I'm not a dream. I'm real, and I'm not going anywhere."

She shook her head. "You and I don't live in the same world. We don't even breathe the same air. You live up there," she waved at the soaring heights of the luxury hotel towering above them, "and I live in a motel with very thin walls."

"It doesn't have to be that way. I want us to try to give this marriage a shot."

The thought of giving up her motel room for his hotel suite was very tempting. But she shook her head. "I serve drinks to the people in your world for a living, Max. I'm invisible to most of them. You actually saw me, and for that I'm very grateful. But that doesn't change the fact that I don't belong in your world."

She stepped into the cab and shut the door firmly in his face. It took all her effort not to look back as the cab pulled out into the traffic.

Chapter Three

Phoenix couldn't wait to get out of her work clothes and into a long hot bath. She'd been on her feet ten hours straight, she was hot, tired, and she couldn't get a certain roguishly charming winemaker out of her thoughts. Even though he hadn't returned her call.

Her mouth watered at the delicious, spicy scent wafting down the motel corridor. It made a pleasant change from the heavy fried grease smell from the apartment next door. The smell would have to keep her going until she'd changed out of her work uniform and ordered take-out.

She slipped her key into the latch and opened the door. The scent wafted straight out of her apartment. She blinked in surprise.

Max stood at the stove she never used, stirring a pot of fragrant...she sniffed the air...Thai curry, with coconut. Yum, another favourite.

"You cook?" Silly question considering what he was doing. Why hadn't she asked the more obvious question of *what are you doing here?* Or better yet: *how did you get in?*

He grinned, and as if reading her thoughts, "Your landlady let me in."

So much for that privacy she'd been promised when she signed the short-term lease.

"Well at least you've saved me a trip." She kicked off her shoes and threw her purse and a large manila envelope onto the white melamine coffee table. "Those are the divorce papers."

Turns out Khara's brother was a divorce lawyer. She'd almost suspected a set-up but her friend had seemed truly contrite.

I can't believe you don't remember she'd said. *It was as if you were under some sort of spell. I was so sure this was it: Love with a capital L.*

That was the champagne, she'd replied.

"You shouldn't have." Max's tone was dry. "Have a bath and I'll pour you some wine."

Too tired to argue, she headed for the bathroom which wasn't much bigger than the closet in his fancy hotel suite. She ground to a halt in the bedroom doorway. A large designer label suitcase lay on the bed. It certainly wasn't hers.

"What the hell is this?" she demanded.

"I told you, I really want us to give this marriage thing a shot and show you that we belong together. Since you don't want to stay with me in my hotel, I checked out and came here."

This was verging on stalkerish. She was sure she should care more but all she could think of was…"There's only one bed."

And he would never fit on the two-seater sofa.

"There was only one bed in my hotel room but that didn't seem to matter."

She wetted her lips. A sane and sensible young woman was not supposed to go weak at the knees at the thought of sharing a bed with her stalker. Nor was she supposed to have fantasies that involved him, her and that same bed.

She pressed her eyes shut.

"You might want to hurry with that bath. Dinner's nearly ready."

She shucked off her clothes as she headed to the bathroom.

Another surprise awaited her there. Steam clung to the walls and frosted the mirror. He'd already run her a bath. Complete with scented oil, rose petals and candles.

All he had to do was throw in the champagne and she'd be screwed. Literally.

She submerged herself in the rose-scented warmth and closed her eyes. Baths, dinner, wine. She could get used to this. If being married meant being waited on hand and foot, then perhaps it wasn't so bad.

Who was she kidding? Everyone she'd ever known who'd married had ended up divorced. Those that made it through, like her parents, and Max's, just landed up with unbearable pain when their partner died. She'd been through that pain twice already and that was more than enough for one lifetime, thank you very much.

When her skin grew wrinkled she finally clambered out the bath. If Max wanted to stick around, then he was about to experience Phoenix as he'd never experienced her before. She grinned as she pulled on her rattiest t-shirt (her father's souvenir of a Megadeth concert a lifetime ago) and her least flattering pair of drawstring sweat pants.

Max had a glass of crisp white wine ready and waiting for her. She took it straight to the couch in front of the television, flopped down, and began to channel surf, deliberately ignoring the table set out ready and waiting. Complete with the crystal vase of yellow roses she'd left in his hotel room.

If she'd hoped to annoy him, it didn't work. He brought his own glass of wine to the sofa and sat beside her. Since it wasn't the largest sofa in the world, his arm slung across the back was as good as slung around her shoulders. She could lean right back into the solid comfort of him…

She shifted as far away as she could.

"If you prefer, we can have dinner on TV trays," he suggested.

She sighed. It was pointless trying to push him away. He invaded her space, her senses, no matter what she did, and an increasingly large part of her enjoyed it.

"The table will be fine." She gulped down a mouthful of wine. "Hey, this is good. Another one of yours?"

His mouth quirked. "Not quite, but it's from my homeland … my father's homeland."

"Where is that?"

He shook his head. "You won't have heard of it. It's a small independent nation called Westerwald."

She hadn't heard of it. "You were born there?"

The television's flicker reflected in his deep azure eyes. "I was raised there."

Which would explain that trace of an accent. "Tell me about it."

He shifted beside her and not entirely coincidentally, his arm slipped around her shoulders. His touch was as good as she remembered.

"The principality is formed around one of Europe's larger rivers. The modern capital is the city of Neustadt, though of course like everything in Europe it's not new at all, but a few centuries old. The city is where the government is based, and the major industries, mainly electronics, but the most beautiful part of the countryside is up river. It's a magical place, rich in folklore and fairy tales, with mountains on either side of the winding river, ancient castles and small medieval towns."

She was fascinated. His voice had taken on a lyrical quality, and she could tell his love for his homeland ran deep. She could picture the place so clearly. She should definitely add this little country she'd never heard of to her Bucket List. "What language do they speak?"

"Since it sits at the crossroads of Europe, the people speak everything. German, French, Dutch, Flemish, and their own dialect.

They even speak English."

Good, then she would be able to get around on her own. Maybe even get a job and stay a while. "You said it's a principality. Does that mean there's a prince?"

"Strictly speaking, it's an arch duchy ruled by the Archduke. But all his sons and grandsons have the title of Prince." He removed his arm from her shoulders and rose. "We should eat before the food gets cold."

She followed him to the table.

The curry was delicious. "Are you this good at everything you do?"

Oops. That wasn't quite what she'd meant to ask, even if it's what she'd been wondering.

He grinned. "I did a cooking tour of Thailand a few summer's ago. Aside from Thai food I can just about scramble an egg."

She laughed. "Then I guess breakfast is my responsibility."

Another oops.

His grin widened. "Was that an invitation to stay the night?"

"Since I don't seem to have any say in the matter, you can stay. But you have to promise to keep to your side of the bed."

"Now where's the fun in that? I thought you were a whole lot more adventurous."

With her mind and body, yes. With her heart? Not so much.

After dinner they curled up together on the sofa and watched mind-numbing TV, not usually Phoenix's entertainment of choice, but it felt surprisingly comforting to just do nothing with Max. Though if he was even half as aware of her as she was of him, then neither of them had a hope in hell of absorbing what they were watching.

Her eyelids began to droop. Two late nights in a row had begun to take their toll.

"Don't fight it," Max said gently. He wrapped her arm around his neck and lifted her off the sofa.

"We're making a bit of a habit of this," she mumbled, as he carried her across the threshold into her narrow bedroom with its beige walls, navy striped curtains, and the same nondescript framed prints that hung in a thousand motel rooms across the country. "I'm sorry. It's nothing like the bed we shared the first night. Not that either of us got much sleep, I think."

"You remember?"

She shook her head wearily against his shoulder. She'd given up trying to remember. It only hurt her head.

He laid her gently on the bed and folded the navy bedspread over her. Then he brushed a kiss across her cheek. She closed her eyes and pretended to sleep.

For a long while she drifted on the edge of sleep, aware of his movements in the other room as he cleared up the remnants of dinner. But she couldn't sleep.

When he finally switched off the television and lights and came into the bedroom, she was wide awake again.

And when he undressed and slid under the sheets beside her, sleep was banished completely. Just great. Tomorrow she'd have to drag herself through another ten hours of fake smiles and exhaustion for more measly tips.

She should have taken one of the sedatives she'd been prescribed after her father's funeral but she no longer trusted them. No longer trusted what she'd do if she took them.

She resolutely turned her back on Max. It made no difference. In the dark, in spite of the television blaring in the apartment on one side and the couple bickering on the other, she was aware of every noise Max made. Of the sound of his breathing, the rustle of sheets as he shifted position, of the creak of the bed when he finally rolled away, giving up on her.

Why was she being such an ass about this? What could it hurt to enjoy having a man in the house? Someone to take care of her and love her.

Someone to make love to her. Her skin prickled at the thought, sending shock waves through her veins.

The answer was out there in the living room, in a thick manila envelope. She had to keep her distance, because she couldn't risk her heart again. She was already bound to him tighter than she wanted. Until he signed those papers, her will was not hers alone. For that reason she couldn't give in to him.

She'd continue to push him away no matter how much it hurt her and no matter how much she wanted him.

She'd rebel against the institution, against the legal binding, as she always had against authority. As her parents had done before her.

If only she and Max were simply two strangers out for a good time, expecting to go their separate ways as soon as the going got tough. *That* she could live with.

She squeezed her eyes shut and begged sleep to take her. But it was a very, very long time before it did.

Waking to the solid warmth of another body in the bed, especially a body that was curled around hers, with an arm slung across her hip, was a novel sensation for Phoenix. In all her living memory, she couldn't remember spooning with anyone. Those rare moments when she lapsed and gave in to her passions, she never hung around long enough to endure the morning after.

Now the morning after didn't seem quite so terrifying. She rolled over in Max's arms, contemplating giving in and cuddling up to that smooth, broad, bare chest. His eyelids fluttered briefly but the real indication that he was awake was the wicked smile that curved his mouth.

She tried to wriggle away, but his arm clamped harder around her, holding her close.

"I offered to make breakfast," she reminded him.

His eyes opened, and she drowned in them. Blue as the sea, infinitely deep, and just as dangerous. "Breakfast can wait. This can't."

His mouth crushed hers, his kiss breathlessly intoxicating. Her entire body responded to his touch, instantly awake and needy. She pressed against him, moulding the length of her body against the hardness and solidness of him.

I shouldn't be doing this. I really *shouldn't be doing this.*

His tongue slid over her parted lips, and she welcomed him in.

He pinned her down and her arms slipped around him, holding him close as if afraid he'd disappear, like the edge of a dream on waking.

This was bad. Already she was afraid of losing him. Already she wanted to cling to him, as if she were drowning.

But she couldn't allow herself to hope. Because if he failed, if the water still claimed either one of them, she'd never recover.

With the last shred of sense left in her, she placed her hands on Max's chest and pushed. Caught unawares, he broke the kiss. But he didn't let her go.

Confusion darkened his eyes. "You don't want…?"

"Yes…no…" Of course she wanted. That was the problem. She extricated herself from his embrace. "I need to think."

"You think too much."

No one had ever accused her of that before. She wasn't exactly a look before you leap kind of person. But she also wasn't the kind of person who was easily led. She made up her own mind and she only ever did what she wanted to do. Which was why her marriage to Max was such a puzzle. She certainly hadn't married against her will, champagne or not.

He tried to pull her back but she resisted, forcing her brightest smile to her face. "I'll make coffee."

45

She was in the kitchen, brewing a pot of coffee, when he wandered through. He still wore nothing but boxers and she was far too aware of that magnificent chest. His shoulders were broad and those abs ... it definitely wasn't the coffee making her mouth water.

She averted her gaze and kept her hands busy filling the kettle. "Hey, the drip's stopped."

"It just needed a washer replacing." Max leaned against the doorjamb.

"You fixed the tap?"

He shrugged, as if it was no big deal. But her estimation of him leapt up another notch. She'd never met a rich man who not only knew how to change a washer, but also didn't mind getting his hands dirty.

She swallowed the lump in her throat. It was real nice having someone take care of her. Even growing up, she'd had to do so much for herself. Dad had been fun and he'd tried hard to make up for the lack of a mother in her life but he was a musician and musos weren't exactly the most practical people she'd ever met. Even the managers and agents who leeched off them tended to be pie-in-the-sky people.

"I'm sure I have eggs and bacon here somewhere. I'll buy some pancake mix tomorrow." She froze. Now where had that come from? Tomorrow? And straight on the heels of that thought came a flash of memory. They'd eaten breakfast together and he'd told her his favourite breakfast was pancakes with blueberries.

Her pulse rate kicked back into gear. Now all she needed was the rest of that day's memories, thank you very much.

She tossed her hair back over her shoulder. If she waited another moment, she wouldn't take the leap. "Tomorrow's my day off. If you want, we can spend it together." She tried to sound off-hand, as if her ability to breathe didn't depend on it.

Max moved behind her. There wasn't much space in the kitchenette. He was sure to hear her heart racing as he stepped close. His hands slipped under the grungy Megadeth t-shirt, smooth and cool against her over-heated skin. The dimple flashed in his cheek as he grinned.

"But I'm still not staying married to you. I don't mind a little fun, but no promises, and definitely no commitments. Okay?"

"Okay." His voice stroked her ear, like a hand brushing velvet. "Does that mean I get to take my wife back to bed now?"

Phoenix glanced at the plastic wall clock. She was still on day shift today but she had a couple of hours yet before she was due at the casino. A couple of hours she could spend running errands. Or making love to Max.

She let out the breath she'd been holding. What the hell. There was only one thing she wanted to do with the next couple of hours, even if it turned out to be yet another mistake in a long line of them.

She laid a hand on his bare chest and felt the rise and fall of his breathing through her fingers. "I have one condition."

He arched an eyebrow.

"No carrying me over the threshold this time."

His grin was feral. "You wanna bet?"

He swept her up. Not into his arms. Not up against his chest. But over his shoulder in a fireman's hold. She laughed and squirmed and beat her fists against his back, but he was far stronger. Over the threshold, into the bedroom, until they both collapsed, laughing and breathless, on the bed.

He stroked her face, roughened fingers brushing her cheek. She turned into his palm and closed her eyes, allowing her other senses free reign as Max trailed a line of kisses down her throat.

His hand slid beneath her t-shirt, sure and steady as he cupped her breast, his thumb brushing over the taut nipple. Sensation flooded her, piercing desire rocketing to her core. He pushed the t-shirt up, over her head, and threw it across the room. His mouth blazed fire down her collarbone, over the curve of her breasts, then he took the other nipple in his mouth, teasing it with his tongue. She moaned and arched her back.

Her whole body was on fire, every inch of her skin sensitised to the rough glide of his skin against hers, his fingers on the peaked nipple of her other breast.

She cried out in dismay when his mouth left her breast but he swallowed the cry with his mouth, kissing her with all the pent-up passion of two days' frustrated want and need. She knew how he felt. Like a volcano, the passion had built inside her from the moment he'd stepped out of that hotel bathroom and stolen her breath away.

Now it was too late to stop. And she really, really didn't want to.

His stubble rasped against her chin, her cheek, her lips, as they kissed. He rolled her over on her back and stripped her pants off without barely even breaking the kiss.

The long hard length of him pressed against her and she arched into him, urging him to take her, to possess her, to complete her, but he had far more control than she did. His hand slid down over her breasts, her stomach and down between her legs.

He unerringly found her sweet spot, circling around the sensitive nub. As his thumb continued its relentless stroke and glide, she widened her legs for him and gasped as he slid his finger into her. The gasp turned into a long, low moan that sounded wild and alien.

"So ready," he murmured against her ear.

She nodded. She was ready.

His fingers moved steadily in and out of her, beating a rhythm in time with the pounding of her blood. She gave herself over to the sensation, abandoned all thought to the tumult of desire rushing through her. Wave upon wave built inside her until she rocked against his hand, crying out as the orgasm crashed through her.

She opened her eyes at last, focussing slowly back on the face that looked steadily down at her. His striking eyes were filled with an emotion so strong that her throat closed. God, to be looked at that way, to be adored like that, was more intoxicating than any drug she'd ever tried. It was more intoxicating even than champagne.

Her limbs still felt heavy and molten as lava. But her desire certainly hadn't cooled. He'd given her a taste and now she was hungry for more. She wanted all of him.

Phoenix rolled him onto his back and sat astride him. "I hope you aren't hungry, because you're not getting breakfast any time soon."

Max laughed, a low, gravelly sound. "Only for you."

She bent and kissed him, a slow, sensuous kiss, less frantic than before, but with no less fervour. His erection pressed against her thigh. Through the fabric of his boxers she held him, rubbing the length of him until he groaned aloud.

"We need protection," he reminded her.

Appalled, she pulled away. She didn't have any protection. She hadn't expected this to happen, certainly hadn't planned for it. Hadn't even given it a moment's thought until now.

"In my wallet." His voice was rough as he struggled up on his elbows. "My pants."

She slid away from him, off the bed, and ransacked the pocket of his pants. She found the wallet in his back pocket, and fumbled for the condom, ignoring the platinum cards and the driver's license. Thank heavens one of them had the foresight to prepare for this.

By the time she returned to the bed and climbed on top of him, he'd shucked off his boxers. She drew in a sharp breath. Clothed, he'd been mouth-wateringly attractive. Naked, he was gorgeous. All lean muscle and smooth planes. She ran an exploring hand down over his chest, over that six pack she'd been itching to touch since they met.

She ripped the packet open with her teeth and with her free hand removed the condom. As she rolled it over the hard, smooth length of him, his erection bucked in her hand. Impatient. As was she.

Their gazes locked together as she lowered herself onto him. She had to admire his strength of will, his control, as he held himself in check, waiting for her to open up to him, to take him in. Only when she'd taken in his full length, did he push up into her, slowly, deliberately.

And that was the last thing they took slowly. She moaned his name and he rolled her over on her back, their bodies still locked together, his hands in her hair. His mouth claimed hers, urgent and fierce with need, and she matched his every move, every thrust of his hips, the ferocious surge as they clawed at each other, merging and tearing apart. Deeper and harder, until her breath came in pants, and she lost awareness of everything but her own pleasure. From a distance, she heard Max call out her name, felt his release inside her. She shattered.

So this was what destiny felt like.

When her breathing returned to normal, she opened her eyes. Tiny aftershocks still radiated through her. Max cradled her in his strong arms, her head against his chest. His heart beat a rapid, staccato rhythm beneath her ear. She lifted her head to look at him. His eyes were hooded but she'd never seen them so blue.

Yes, she had.

She fumbled at the memory, grasped it. The first time they'd made love, he'd looked at her like that. That first time he'd taken it slow. He'd made her keep her eyes open so he could watch her climax. And it had been unlike anything she'd ever experienced before. It had overtaken her so thoroughly, blown her whole being apart and reconstructed her again. Afterwards, he'd held her exactly as he held her right now and she'd felt like a new person, more alive than she'd ever felt.

Happier than she'd ever felt.

And she hadn't minded at all that she'd been wearing his ring. Or that she'd given up her freedom to be with him. Or her stubble burn.

She pulled out of Max's embrace. "The coffee must be cold by now," she said. "I'll need to make a fresh pot."

He let her go, leaning up on his elbow to watch as she pulled on her over-sized t-shirt. "Remind me to buy you something a little sexier for bed." His lips quirked on the edge of one of his mesmerising grins.

She glanced down at the shirt. "It was supposed to be a deterrent." A fat lot of good it had done. She should have known it would take more than a ratty old t-shirt to stop a volcano.

She headed for the kitchen, keeping herself busy with pans and plates, and trying to ignore the sound of water running in the shower or the image in her head of him naked under the spray.

It was a crappy shower, nowhere near as nice as the massaging jets in the enormous shower cubicle of his fancy hotel. And there definitely wasn't space for two in this one, so she could just get *that* image out of her head.

He emerged from the shower smelling of her floral and very feminine shampoo. He wrapped an arm around her waist and kissed the back of her neck as she laid the table. Her stomach growled and she playfully swatted him away. "I need sustenance."

They ate quickly, feeding their basic needs so they could get back to an even more basic one. She finished her coffee sitting in his lap, unable to keep away from him a moment longer, needing to touch him and be touched. He was a magnet, drawing her in, and she had no choice but to give in to the thrall.

She could only pray that when the spell broke, as it inevitably would, there wouldn't be tears. The one consolation was that she wouldn't be the one crying. She hadn't cried since she was ten and if she hadn't cried for her father, she sure as hell wasn't going to cry over losing any other man.

Chapter Four

Mondays were Phoenix's day off, the days she got to do whatever she wanted. She lay on her side, head propped on her arm and watched as Max woke. He stretched like a panther; one toned, glorious limb after another. Then he opened his eyes. It was incredible that even after waking beside him for several days, the colour of his eyes still startled her.

How one pair of eyes could be so aware and intelligent, so twinkling, and so seductive all at the same time was truly unfair to every other man out there. And if women didn't fall instantly in love with his eyes, then there was his body too...

Though he no doubt had his pick of any woman he wanted, he'd chosen *her*. She still had no memory of what she'd done to inspire that interest, but who was she to complain?

He rolled on his side, mirroring her position, and smiled. "What do you want to do today?"

And that voice! It rolled seductively down her spine, setting her alight.

"I've had my turn. What have you always wanted to do in Vegas? You didn't come all this way with the sole purpose of getting married, I hope." That would be way beyond stalkerish and straight into insanity.

He grinned, a slow, heated curve of that sensual mouth. "No. Same as everyone else, I came here to get drunk, throw away a lot of money gambling and find a beautiful woman to spend my winnings on. Two out of three isn't bad."

"So today we go gambling?"

He chuckled, low and seductive. "I didn't get drunk the day we married. I knew exactly what I was doing. No, there's only one thing I want to do today." He ran his palm down her shoulder, over her breasts … she moaned … to settle on her hip. "I'd like to stay in bed."

She gave him a gentle shove. "What a waste of a good day. Besides, there must be plenty of women in Napa dying to let you between their legs, so why come all the way to Vegas for that?"

His eyes darkened. They did that, she noticed, every time she didn't know something he'd already told her that first day they'd spent together. Tough. She only gave herself a headache if she tried to remember that day.

She slid away from his hand and out the bed, pulling on her loose kimono-style wrap. "You might want to spend the day in bed but I have laundry to do and groceries to buy."

He leaned back on the pillows, arms behind his head. The sheet only covered so much and she had to avert her eyes to resist leaping straight back into the bed with him.

"If you tear up those divorce papers and come to California with me, you'd never have to do laundry again."

"Tempting as your offer is, no thanks."

"Why not?" He sat up, eyes flashing. Frustration rolled off him in angry waves. "What is so wrong with being married to me?"

"It's nothing personal. I don't want to be tied to one person for the rest of my life. What if I meet someone else?"

"You won't." The cocky grin was back, the frustration wiped

away by that infernal cheerful confidence.

"You think you've spoiled me for every other man? You're either seriously arrogant or seriously deluded, Farm Boy."

"No, I just know that destiny has brought us together. We can't fight it."

She damned well intended to try. She didn't believe in destiny. She turned on her heel and stalked to the kitchen. Max was nuts. Sexy as sin, but nuts.

He called after her. "I know you're afraid, Phoenix. But your courage is bigger than your fear."

He had to get in the last word, didn't he? She gritted her teeth and switched on the kettle.

It was impossible to stay angry at him, though. After he'd patiently accompanied her to the Laundromat, carried her groceries, and even fixed the dodgy handle on her closet door, she could hardly kick him out.

And then there was the comic entertainment he provided. Their bus ride had been particularly amusing.

"Have you seriously never travelled on a bus before?"

"How could you tell?" He might have looked sheepish if his dimple hadn't emerged. Instead, he was mischief personified.

"Oh, I don't know. The way you flagged it down like a cab, and then told the driver exactly where you wanted to go."

"How else will he know where we're going?"

She laughed. "He couldn't give a toss where we're going. He's a municipal employee, and all he cares about is his pay check at the end of the month. It's up to us to know where we're going."

"You know if you stayed married to me, you'd never have to ride a bus again either," he muttered. She pretended not to hear him.

What she couldn't ignore was the white-hot chemical reaction that ignited when the bus lurched and she rocked against Max.

With his free hand, he steadied her, holding him against her in an embrace far too intimate for the public setting. Heat rushed through her veins and she found herself unable to pull away.

Then his lips came down on hers, and all she could do to remain standing was to wrap her arms around Max and cling to him.

"Get a room," a voice muttered.

"Good idea," Max whispered in her ear.

They barely got through the front door before they'd torn their clothes off and he had her unceremoniously on her back on the kitchen table.

He made up for the lightning speed of that coupling the next time round, taking it so tantalisingly slow that it was even more incredible than the last.

Forget laundry and buses. She could seriously get used to *this*.

"It's nothing more than sex." Phoenix loaded up her tray with soda cans and high ball glasses full of ice. A week's worth of the most incredible sex imaginable. Just thinking about Max made her hot, and more than a little breathless.

Khara giggled, her voice barely pitched above the constant din of the slot machines. "Yes, but what sex! Can you think of any better reason to stay married?"

"It won't last." But even as she said the words, Phoenix had to admit she didn't want it to end. Max hadn't signed the divorce papers yet. And neither had she.

Maybe being married to Max wasn't such a bad thing after all. Maybe Napa would be a very pleasurable adventure. And when it stopped being pleasurable...well, there'd be time enough to sign the papers then.

She could write this marriage off as an adventure. And then she'd go off on her trip around the world. Or maybe...what if Max went with her?

The trip would be much more fun shared with someone who made her laugh, someone who made her feel safe and protected when she lay in his arms, someone who set her body alight with nothing more than a touch.

No, better not think of that. Especially now, when she had thirsty gamblers to serve and an uptight boss to keep happy.

Napa would be a very pleasant change from this. She could see herself drinking wine on a verandah overlooking a vineyard. Even if she had to serve her own drinks, it would sure beat getting stuck here in Vegas.

She smiled. She'd tell Max her decision tonight. She itched for her shift to end, counting the minutes as they slowly ticked away.

Max scowled and looked up from his laptop at the urgent banging on the door. It was hard enough to concentrate on the vineyard's sales data and marketing charts with the noise coming through the walls from the neighbours (did they have to keep the TV volume so high?) without some cold caller at the door.

Since the knocking refused to go away, he rose and crossed to the door, slamming it open without first checking the peephole.

"What are you doing here?"

Westerwald's prime minister wrinkled his nose and looked around. "I'd ask you the same question but the landlady already made the answer quite clear." His expression said it all. He thought Max was here for sex. Though he wasn't entirely wrong, the contempt on the older man's face had Max's hands fisting at his sides.

Two bodyguards in ominous black suits and sunglasses flanked his visitor.

Max leaned against the doorjamb, irritation levels climbing another notch. If Albert intended on making any disparaging remarks about Phoenix or where she lived, Max would give him the boot. Literally. They were on his turf here, not Albert's. "Okay, let me re-phrase. What do you want?"

"Are you alone?" Albert had been a member of the cabinet for close to a decade, and a smooth politician for many years before that. In all that time, Max had never seen him display emotion. The anxious look the man cast about him now was the closest Max had ever seen him get to flustered.

"I am."

Albert ran a hand through his short salt-and-pepper hair, making it stand on end. "May I please come in?"

Albert was always calm and unflappable; he wouldn't let even a little desert heat interfere with his deportment. Max, in cargo shorts and a golf shirt, felt over-heated, so it was no wonder the older man in his usual three-piece suit, was beginning to look like a tomato. A harried tomato.

Max took pity on him and stepped aside. "You can come in but your goons can go play somewhere else. I don't want anyone here asking questions."

Albert nodded at the chief goon and stepped inside. He eyed the sofa with distaste, but sat anyway.

Max closed the door and remained standing. "Are you here in Vegas for business or pleasure?" Hardly the latter, since the cabinet no doubt had its hands full breaking in their new constitutional monarch.

He grinned. He had a pretty good idea the hoops Rik was making them jump through. When they were younger they'd shared lengthy debates on what needed to be done to bring Westerwald into the 21st century. Rik must be in his element.

"You didn't reply to my emails." The cabinet minister frowned. "I tried to call you, but your phone was off and at the vineyard they refused to tell me where you are. Your grandfather is most obstinate."

"I switched my cell phone off and Grandfather was only following my instructions." Max crossed his arms over his chest. Enough small talk. "How did you find me?"

"I asked the secret service to track your IP address. I think that's the right terminology." Max hadn't even known Westerwald had a secret service. But before he could open his mouth to ask why Albert had gone to such lengths, the other man waved an agitated hand and interrupted. "We have a crisis. I didn't know what else to do. We need you in Westerwald before the newspapers hit the streets tomorrow."

"Shouldn't you be going to my brother with this?"

"We don't know where he is."

Max's eyebrows shot up. This was news. And perhaps went a way to explaining why the prime minister of Westerwald himself was here instead of some flunky. "You could track me down, but you don't know where Rik is? Did you look inside the palace?"

Albert's expression turned apoplectic. "This isn't a joke. Your brother has run away. Not that I blame him but we need to have you briefed and standing in front of the television cameras in the palace audience chamber at ten o'clock tomorrow morning."

What the hell? Max did a rapid mental calculation. It was midday in Nevada. Taking time zones into account, they'd only make it if they left right now.

He sucked in a deep breath. This clearly wasn't a joke, and if Albert didn't calm down soon, he was going to have a heart attack.

"Do you want a glass of water, or tea? Then you can tell me what this is all about."

"Water, please."

Max fetched a bottle of water from the refrigerator, handed it to Albert, and then sat on the melamine coffee table across from the older man. Once Albert had taken a few long gulps of the cool water, he returned to his usual phlegmatic politician's expression.

But not without effort.

"I'm not sure if you know this, but as soon as DNA testing became scientifically accepted, it was written into our constitution that all Archdukes would be tested on accession."

Max nodded. It was just like the scandal-fearing government to cover their asses, but it was a formality and no big deal.

"There was an irregularity with your brother's test." Albert looked away, unable to conceal his embarrassment. "We checked it twice before we spoke with Prince Fredrik."

A slice of cold shivered down Max's back. "What was the irregularity?"

"Prince Fredrik is not after all your father's son, it seems."

Silence fell. Albert shifted uncomfortably on the sofa.

Max had no idea how long he stared at the man before the words actually made any sense. "Are you sure of this?"

"The prince...your brother...went to talk to your mother. We haven't seen him since, and your mother has locked herself in her private apartment and refuses to talk to anyone."

My God.

Max dropped his head into his hands. Could it be possible? Had his mother cheated on their father? The mental calculations kept coming. Rik had been a honeymoon baby, and premature on top of that.

Those were the oldest excuses in the book, weren't they? Had his father known the bride he'd fallen in love with was pregnant with another man's child?

He rubbed his face. No, his father had most certainly not known. He'd always prized Westerwald's honour above his own. He'd never have raised Rik to take over the reins if he'd known he wasn't a blood heir.

He'd have raised Max to do it instead.

He lifted his head. "What do you need me to do?"

"We have a press conference booked for ten tomorrow. There have already been rumours and there's not much we can do to stop the press speculation. What we need to do now is damage control. We need to assure the press and the public that there will be no disruption to the nation. That you will take your father's place as Archduke and life carries on the same in Westerwald. And somehow prevent your family's name from being dragged any further through the mud."

Life carries on the same ... not for Rik that was for sure. His heart contracted at the thought of what his brother must be going through right now.

And not for him either. In the space of a heartbeat, nothing in Max's life would ever be the same again. He needed to come clean with Phoenix and he needed to do it *now*.

He rose and began to search for his cell phone. "How soon can we fly?"

"The jet is fuelled and ready at the airport. Customs and passport control are standing by so we can leave immediately."

Max nodded. The cell phone was in the side pocket of his laptop bag. It took precious minutes to switch on. With agitated fingers he dialled Phoenix's number.

It went straight to voice mail. Damn. Of course it would. Her boss didn't allow the staff to keep their cell phones on at work. He listened to her voice, until the beep sounded.

What should he say?

There was a lot he needed to say, but none of it could be left in a voice message.

"Call me the moment you get this message." He cut off the call. Not nearly enough.

He glanced at the wall clock. She'd be at work for another three hours. They could drive past the casino where she worked...but that would take time. Time they didn't have.

He'd have to leave a note. He pulled the memo pad and pen from beside the phone.

"We don't have time for this," Albert snapped impatiently. "The car is waiting, and we're already behind schedule."

"Pack my bag while I write."

It was a measure of how serious the situation was that the most senior cabinet minister of a European nation accepted the order without hesitation. Max was sure the British prime minister would never have packed the Queen's suitcase. He swallowed his laughter. Not the time, nor the place.

He concentrated on the note.

I have a family crisis I have to attend to, but I'll call as soon as I can. Whatever you do, please don't file those papers. I'll explain everything soon. I love you.

He signed it Max. That would have to do for now.

From his laptop case he removed an envelope with the Mandarin Oriental's embossed logo. He folded the note and slipped it inside, then reached into his pocket and pulled out his signet ring. The antique Westerwald heirloom his father had given him on his eighteenth birthday, one of only three ever made.

He sealed the ring into the envelope, set the key Phoenix had given him on top of it, packed up his laptop, and did a quick sweep of the rooms to make sure Albert hadn't missed anything. Then he crossed to the door, flipped the latch, and pulled the door shut behind him.

The click of the latch as it locked had a resoundingly final ring to it.

Phoenix hopped off the bus and hurried down the street towards the motel. She hummed as she walked. She had only known Max for a week and he'd turned her life upside down and inside out, and she was *humming*.

Tonight she would tell him her decision to go to Napa with him. After all, what was keeping her in Vegas? A dead-end job with a boss who had no sense of humour whatsoever?

She'd already handed in her notice and she was free as a bird.

At the apartment door, she fished her cell phone out of her bag as well as the keys. Still no response from Max. She'd called as soon as she got off shift and picked up his message, but his phone was switched off as usual. In her world, most people needed to be surgically detached from their phones. It was yet another indication of how far apart their lives were. Max never seemed to switch his on.

She slid the key into the lock and smiled as she turned it. But perhaps after all there was a strong enough connection between their worlds that they could overcome their differences. Max was right. This was more than just lust between them. Lust alone wouldn't have kept her smiling like a loon all day. She wasn't yet ready to use the other L word, but maybe…

The apartment was empty. No fancy dinner or candle-lit baths tonight, clearly. Perhaps he planned to take her out for dinner instead.

"Max?" she called, throwing her purse down on the sofa and moving to the bedroom. Also empty. It was only when she reached the bathroom that the fear began to bubble in the pit of her stomach.

His toothbrush was gone.

She strode back into the bedroom and flung open his cupboard. Empty.

Fear lanced through her, pain sharp and familiar, and so dizzying she had to steady herself against the door.

She hurried back to the living room, moving so quickly she stubbed her toe on the edge of the sofa. But the pain was nothing to the stabbing pain in her heart as she spotted the key.

She couldn't breathe.

Sucking in gulps of air, she sank onto the sofa.

Max was gone. Like everyone else in her life, he was gone.

The tide engulfed her and she fought against it. She wasn't going to let herself go down. No-one was going to pull her down to that dark place again.

She raised her head. So what? So what that Max had failed her? She'd always known it was going to end eventually – that either he would leave or she would. This was what she'd wanted, right? To end things before they got complicated.

Except that it was already complicated.

She picked up the envelope beneath the key. It lay thick and heavy in her hand. With fingers that were steadier than they had any right to be, she slit open the envelope and gasped.

Hundred dollar bills. Lots of them. And a note.

She unfolded the note, laughing hollowly as she read Max's large, neat handwriting.

I love you. Yeah, right.

He loved her enough to pay her off like some harlot. One abrupt voice message, and then he'd switched off his bloody phone.

He knew where she worked. If he'd truly cared he could have told her face-to-face before he left, but no, he'd left a three line note and cash.

She removed the cash and flicked through it. Enough for a plane ticket out of here. She didn't really care where she was going as long as it was far away from Vegas. There were memories here now that she didn't want to re-visit.

There was still something stuck inside the envelope. She gave it a shake and Max's ring fell out onto her palm. A keepsake, how nice. At least the ring made her feel a little less like a whore being paid for services rendered.

She rolled the ring over and over between her fingers. She'd keep it. She'd keep it real close where it could serve as a reminder of what happened when you let people close, when you let them into your heart.

She was never going to be suckered into that again.

Stuffing the cash back into the envelope, she grabbed the key and headed for the door. It was after normal working hours but in this town there was guaranteed to be a travel agent somewhere who could advise her how far away she could get on three thousand dollars.

There was no point in looking back. It was time to move forward.

Chapter Five

Max's gaze drifted out the tall arched windows of the council room. Rain battered against the windows. God, but he missed the clear blue Californian sky.

He refused to think of the other things he missed. He'd only drive himself crazy.

"If that's all gentlemen, then I'll see you all at the coronation?" Albert's dry voice cut through the fog of his thoughts. The other members of the cabinet murmured their assent and the meeting drew to a close. Papers rustled and chairs scraped on the hard-wood floors.

Max stretched and rose from his chair, knotted muscles protesting, and turned to Albert, seated on his right. "May I have a private word?"

"Of course, Your Highness."

He still wasn't used to being addressed this way. 'Your Highness' had been his father. In Napa, even the migrant farm workers had called him Max. 'Your Highness' made him feel old. He felt old a lot these days.

"I want to make a slight change to the coronation plans."

Albert nodded, not quite able to hide his look of resignation.

If he'd hoped Max would be a more pliable Archduke than Rik, he'd been sorely mistaken. In the two months they'd worked side by side, or more appropriately head to head, he'd had plenty of time to learn that while Max had not been raised to be the ruling Prince, he had strong ideas on what he wanted and a stubborn insistence on getting it.

And what Max wanted right now, he knew Albert wasn't going to like. "I've decided that the coronation should be held in Waldburg."

Albert choked. "You can't be serious. Neustadt is our capital. The coronations always take place in the cathedral here."

"Not always." Max smothered a smile. No-one knew their country's history better than he did. They were more than bedtime tales for him. These were the stories of his ancestors. "Waldburg was the seat of Westerwald's power for a thousand years. Until the nineteenth century, every coronation was held in the castle at Waldburg. I want to return to that tradition."

"But the church there will never hold all the dignitaries we've invited. And what about the public who will want to be there to celebrate the day?"

He'd grown up in the small medieval walled town on the banks of the Wester River. Everyone there knew him and those were the people he wanted around him when he pledged his life away, not a bunch of strangers. "There'll be TV cameras broadcasting live. And those people who want to can travel to Waldburg. We'll lay on buses and boats."

Albert pressed his lips together. "I think this is a very bad idea. Your coronation is mere weeks away and the arrangements have all been made."

"Then unmake them." Max drew in a deep breath. He hadn't been sleeping well lately, but that was no excuse for winding up the people's elected leader. "You are a meticulous planner, with a very capable support staff. I have no doubt you will be able to make the necessary arrangements. But the coronation will take place in the same place where my ancestors were crowned."

Albert bowed and began to withdraw.

"And one more thing." Max leached the emotion from his voice. "That matter I asked the secret service to look into...?"

Albert would not look him in the eye. "There has been no news. There's been no word of her since she landed in Madrid."

Max's hands fisted as he fought back the anger. He had no one to blame but himself. He should have found her. He should not have left without talking to her.

But there'd been no time.

As it was, he'd walked into the press conference late. He'd walked straight into turmoil, and it still wasn't over. Two months was not yet long enough for people to forget the salacious headlines. Rik was lying low somewhere avoiding the press, and their mother had escaped back to her childhood home in California. Max only wished he could do the same. He hadn't truly appreciated what he'd had in his old life until it was irretrievably gone.

Instead, he was stuck here, fixing everyone else's problems, alone.

The republicans' calls to abolish the monarchy were louder than ever, the paparazzi stalked his every move, and no-one called him by his given name any more. And the worst of it was he could see no way out. No way back to the place he wanted to be or the person he wanted to be.

"Might I make a suggestion, Your Highness?"

He forced the darkness away and turned back to Albert with a brisk nod.

"Forget about her. There will be other women, far more suitable women."

His eyes narrowed but he said nothing.

"Is there anything else, Your Highness?"

He shook his head. "You may go."

Left alone in the vast council chamber, with its ornate gilded ceiling and wainscoted walls, Max wandered across to the high windows. The palace gardens lay below, now blurred behind a veil of rain. The formal garden led down in terraces to an artificial lake, which separated the Baroque palace from the equally formal town. Everything here was neat and organised, the streets laid out on a grid pattern, row after row of identical grey buildings.

He hated the city.

But now that the government had broken for the summer he was free at last to go home. To Waldburg, to the rambling castle overlooking the river and the vineyards. Waldburg, where castle and town lay intertwined and people he'd known all his life still called him 'Max'. Now that his own family were gone, he longed to see even one friendly face.

His heart ached but he pushed the emotion away. He needed to focus on what had to be done. He needed not to feel.

At least in Waldburg, away from the endless meetings and duties and the need to put everyone else first, he hoped to be able to sleep again. He hadn't slept well in two months, not without waking from tortured dreams to find himself alone in a vast canopied bed in a strange room.

Perhaps in Waldburg he'd be able to make sense of his life. Of the secrets and lies that made a mockery of everything he'd ever believed in.

His mother had been unfaithful to his father and their life together had been built on lies. Phoenix hadn't cared enough to wait. Overnight, she'd dumped her cell phone and left the country.

Truth, destiny, true love – were they all a sham? He sighed and twisted away from the window. It seemed, increasingly, that every belief he'd held onto was nothing more than an illusion.

Phoenix placed an upturned chair on an empty table and continued to sweep. Her new boss, a young woman not much older than herself, entered the café from the kitchen. "You sure you don't mind locking up for me tonight?"

Phoenix shook her head. "I'll be fine. You go out and have some fun."

Rebekah was newly married but she and her husband hardly had time together since he worked at the castle, and coronation preparations were taking his every spare moment. Phoenix had timed her arrival perfectly. Rebekah had been so desperate for extra help she'd overlooked the fact that Phoenix had no work permit. The job came with a tiny apartment too, which was just as well since the trip through Spain and France had pretty much wiped out her savings and the cash from Max.

Before she arrived in Westerwald, she'd got down to thinking of Max only about a dozen times a day. Was he back in Napa, making wines and rejoicing in his narrow escape from marriage? Or did he miss her?

But here in Westerwald she thought of him all the time. The moment she'd heard of a town with his name, she'd come straight here. She'd loved the rugged mountains of Spain, but here in the town of Waldburg she'd fallen in love with the vineyard-clad green hills on either side of the wide river and the town of half-timbered houses that clustered around the romantic castle. Even the town square with its giant fountain, where Rebekah's café was situated, had a fairy tale quality to it.

Everywhere she turned here she was reminded of him, of the tales he'd told her.

She swept vigorously, not seeing what she was doing.

Had Max signed and filed the papers she'd sent to the vineyard? She hoped so. She hoped he'd moved on and that he was happy. Really, she did.

Even if, in the darkness and quiet of her room at night, the anger still festered that he'd left her. Or worse, those nights when the anger turned to grief, brutally reminding her that she was alone and that she could rely on no-one – that she had to find her joy in whichever way she could. Those were the nights she found the loudest, liveliest club in town and partied until dawn.

She brushed away the dark mood, and bent down to lift another chair and set it on a table-top. The chain around her neck swung loose of her shirt. She stuffed it back.

"What is that?" Rebekah asked.

"It's nothing. A souvenir."

"May I see it?"

Phoenix held up the chain and the ring that dangled from the end of it.

Rebekah stepped close to look, holding the ring reverently. "It's a very good copy. It almost looks real."

Whatever did she mean? "It is real, I think." Phoenix frowned. "Actually, I don't know much about it. A friend gave it to me."

Rebekah pressed her lips together, expression thoughtful.

Phoenix slipped the ring back where it belonged, over her heart. "I wear it to remind me not to get too attached to anyone or anything."

Rebekah frowned. "Why?"

"Because the man who gave it to me walked out without even saying goodbye. Because nothing ever lasts."

"You're in the wrong place for that, then."

"What do you mean?"

"This castle, and the town and nation that's grown around it, is more than a thousand years old, and still ruled by the descendants of the first nobleman who claimed this land for himself. Here, everything lasts."

She couldn't even comprehend a family with a thousand year

history. She'd never even met her grandparents. Phoenix sighed. "Things, places, but not people."

"One day you'll find that someone meant just for you and it will last."

"Does everyone in this country believe in fairy tales?" Phoenix rolled her eyes.

Rebekah laughed softly. "What is wrong with believing in fairy tales?" She laid her hand on Phoenix's arm. "I hope for your sake you find that someone soon. It must be very lonely not having someone to love."

Loneliness was a whole lot easier to deal with than loss.

"Go on, or you're going to be late for your date with your husband." She gave Rebekah a gentle shove towards the door. "And I can't clean the floor with you standing on it."

Rebekah chuckled and headed out the door with a wave. Phoenix set to work sweeping the floor. The mindless task gave her thoughts chance to roam, back to a motel apartment in Vegas, or even further, to that vineyard in Napa she'd never seen but could picture so perfectly.

She brushed aside the twinge of regret and focussed back on the task at hand. There was no point dwelling on the past. What was done, was done, and she was moving forward.

"It's so good to have you home again."

Max clasped his one-time playmate's hand. "It's good to be back. I've been away far too long." He looked around the sunlit solar, once the private chamber of the medieval royal household. Lunch had been set ready for him on the long polished wooden table. A place for one.

He was sick and tired of eating alone, and even more tired of servants who eyed him suspiciously if he tried to start a conversation. Claus didn't drop his gaze or leave a room backwards, and Max wanted to keep him talking with a need bordering on desperation. "You're in charge here since your father retired?"

"Yeah. Unlike you, I never wanted to leave. I'm more than happy being the third generation steward of the castle."

"I'll gladly swap your job for mine. Though I'm sure you're under a lot of pressure at the moment, what with the arrangements for the coronation. I'm sorry about that, but we had to do it in a hurry."

"I hear the republican party have called for a referendum."

Max nodded. "They'd have loved to postpone the coronation until after the vote. Their argument is that it's a waste of state funds and if Westerwald gets rid of its monarchy, then the tax payers will be saved a great deal of money. They have a point, but Albert was adamant we get the coronation over and done with before the government re-opens after the summer."

Claus grinned. "I agree. And since I'll be out of a job if there's no more monarchy, I'd better get back to work making this the best damned coronation in history. I've a meeting scheduled with the TV people to work out how they're going to place their cameras in a medieval church that wasn't designed for such things."

Great. Another responsibility on his shoulders. Max owed it to all those people like Claus who depended on the monarchy for their jobs to make this coronation so spectacular (on a limited budget, of course) that the population would vote to keep him in power.

There were days he wished he could do what Phoenix had done – just up and leave and go exploring. There were even days he couldn't give a toss what happened to the people of Westerwald.

He could be back in Napa cultivating new wines. Or in Spain, searching for Phoenix.

He shook his head. She'd done such a fantastic disappearing act, that she obviously didn't want to be found. So much for better or for worse.

He shut down that line of thought. Albert was right. He should forget her. But memory had never been *his* problem.

And thinking of wives and weddings… "I hear congratulations are in order, and that you married recently."

Claus' face lit up as he smiled. "I did."

Max's heart lurched. He envied his friend's joy. He'd known that happiness for scarcely a week before he'd lost it. He forced a smile. "Anyone I know?"

"Rebekah. She was in school with us."

"Pig tails and freckles? Her parents owned the café on the square where we used to get ice creams after school?"

Claus laughed. "The café's still there but Rebekah runs it now." Max grinned. "And she doesn't have pig tails anymore."

Max had spent the first years of his schooling in a local school right here in Waldburg. His mother had insisted on keeping her children close. That changed when his grandfather died and his father acceded as head of state. They'd moved to the city, and he and Rik transferred to an elite private school. But they'd still spent their summers here in Waldburg and the friendships forged in those halcyon younger days had remained strong.

Claus clapped Max on the back and headed for the door. "If you need anything, just ring the bell. The housekeeping staff are standing by. Your wish is their command." He paused in the doorway, suddenly serious. "I can't believe I nearly forgot… you know the Waldburg rings?" he sucked in a breath, clearly unsure what to say next.

Max nodded to him to go on.

"My father told me one of the rings went missing more than thirty years ago and hasn't been seen since."

Max nodded more slowly this time. He and Rik had been given the remaining rings on their eighteenth birthdays. The third ring had already been long gone by that time. In fact, the missing ring had become something of a family legend.

Or perhaps not a legend but another family secret.

"Rebekah thinks she might have seen it. She has a young woman working for her who has a ring like yours and Rik's."

A shiver chased down Max's spine. There'd been rumours about what had happened to the third ring, each more implausible than the last. Was it possible it might finally be found and the mystery solved?

Though he wasn't entirely sure he wanted to know the answers. His family already had more skeletons in the closet than he'd ever suspected and he didn't think he could deal with any more right now.

"Thank you for letting me know," he said.

"See you later." Claus' cheerful farewell was a world away from the cabinet ministers' formal bows. Max stretched his shoulders and felt a little of his tension dissipate.

He didn't have time to go unravelling family mysteries anyway. He had a coronation to prepare, a mutiny to quell, and a frenzied media to suppress. That was enough for this week, thank you.

The royal family's private apartments were naturally on the farthest side of the castle from the town, in the wing that overlooked the sloping vineyards rather than the river. It was quiet here, reminding Max far too much of the quiet of his grandfather's sprawling, comfortable farmhouse back in Napa and making sleep even more impossible.

He gave up tossing restlessly in the enormous bed, threw off the sheets and began to dress. Usually when sleep eluded him, he burned off his frustrations in the gym. But unlike the palace at Neustadt, this castle had no private gym. He'd have to walk off his mood instead.

He threw on dark jeans and a black shirt and headed out.

The main entrance was well guarded and Security was no doubt under strict instructions to provide him with a bodyguard wherever he went. Since Max had no intention of being tailed as he walked, especially in this dark mood, he went downstairs to the kitchens instead. A single bulb burned low in the vast, empty kitchen.

There was a small unsecured casement window in one of the old pantries that overlooked the service lane leading to the now disused coal sheds. As kids, he and Rik had used it as an escape route out of the castle. Max prayed the window hadn't been fitted with bars anytime in the last twenty years.

It hadn't.

He slid open the window, holding his breath as the mechanism squealed in protest, then he leaned out to check the coast was clear. The lane was empty, so he squeezed out through the opening. It wasn't as easy as it once was, but he managed to wriggle through and caught a low-hanging branch of the ancient tree that shielded the lane. At least the drop on the other side was shorter than he remembered.

He pushed the window shut, leaving enough of a gap so he could pry it open when he returned, and strode whistling down the deserted cobbled street, hands in his pockets, feeling free for the first time in months.

For the first time since he'd made that mad dash from Las Vegas.

A brisk wind blew between the buildings. Closer to the town square, the streets were more brightly lit and less eerily quiet, but many of the buildings were in darkness, the residents tucked in behind their shuttered windows for the night.

Waldburg was a sleepy town. Its one and only night club seldom stayed open past midnight. But it was a balmy summer's night and the town's population had doubled in anticipation of the coronation, or so the Minister of Tourism had informed him this morning. So he wasn't entirely surprised to see a couple of restaurants around the town square still lit up, music playing, and people milling about the central fountain.

None of the revellers paid him the least attention. Clearly no one expected the nation's new Archduke to be wondering the streets alone late at night.

Rebekah's family café was closed though. The red and white striped awning was new, the painted sign on the windows fresh, and the tables and chairs outside had been packed away for the night, but it hadn't changed.

A dim light burned inside, the kind of light that might be left on at night for security. As he was about to turn away, a figure crossed in front of it. Good, they were still up. Perhaps Claus and Rebekah would invite him in for a friendly drink. He was tired of being alone.

He hurried across the square to knock on the café door. There was no answer, so he tried the handle. The door opened. Security didn't seem an issue for the locals.

The figure in the kitchen moved again. A woman, with hair tied up in a swinging pony tail, carrying a tray of wine glasses that refracted the light as she moved. For a moment, as her silhouette caught the light, his heart seized. Not Rebekah. But could it be possible?

The blood slammed through him and he knew that it was.

Not the third ring at all. Just the one he'd left behind in a bland motel room in Vegas.

Thank you, Destiny. He grinned, his faith restored for the first time in months.

Chapter Six

The sound of footsteps in the café startled Phoenix and she nearly dropped the wine glasses she'd been unpacking from the dishwasher.

"Who's there?" she called, turning to face the intruder. A man leaned in the darkened doorway, and for a second, her heart jumped. Then reason kicked in. She must be imagining things. Clearly a long day on her feet had taken its toll. She set down the glasses and rubbed her eyes.

"Phoenix?"

There was no denying the voice, though. Her hands started to shake.

"What are you doing here?" he asked.

For a mad moment, she wondered how he'd managed to track her down. But of course he hadn't. This was a coincidence and nothing more.

Destiny, a small voice whispered. She shook her head. She didn't believe in destiny. She believed in making her own destiny.

"Cleaning up."

He leaned against the doorjamb, crossing his arms over that broad chest. "I meant what are you doing in Waldburg?"

She steadied her voice. "I heard there was going to be a coronation and thought it sounded like fun. What are *you* doing here?"

His smile was more mocking than amused. "I'm here for the coronation too." He pushed away from the doorjamb. "I asked you to wait for me."

"I didn't think you'd come back."

"I'm a man of my word and you didn't even give me a chance to prove it. Exactly how long did you wait? Two hours, three?"

Even in this dim light she could see that the usual amusement was absent from his eyes. There was a new expression there, hard and cold. His once shaggy hair was cut short and neat, and he looked more formidable than the surfer boy he'd appeared when they first met.

This wasn't the careless, happy-go-lucky Max she'd met in Vegas. He was serious and intense, and there were worry lines in his forehead that hadn't been there before.

How could he have changed so much in two months? Surely her leaving couldn't have changed him that much? She cleared her throat. "Twelve."

"Twelve hours." He walked slowly closer and she backed against the counter top. There was nowhere else to go.

"I tried to call. Your phone was off." Again. "And I wasn't going to sit around waiting for you to deign to call." At least not after the first eight excruciating hours of waiting.

"It might interest you to know that twelve hours after I left I was still in mid-air. Most airlines discourage the use of cell phones mid-flight."

"And I tried to call the vineyard where you said you worked, only they said they'd never heard of you."

His jaw tightened. "My grandfather's very protective of me."

"No kidding." She crossed her arms over her chest. He had a cheek putting her on the defensive. Okay, so he had explanations for not taking her calls. And she had been hasty. Didn't mean she had to cut him any slack. "Did you get your family business sorted?"

"More or less."

More or less? What kind of an answer was that? He knew everything there was to know about her, for heaven's sake. He'd insisted they were soul mates but he still wouldn't give her straight answers. She set her hands on her hips. "What did you do with the divorce papers?"

He frowned. "What do you mean? I left them right where you did – on the dresser."

"I mailed them to you at the vineyard and asked you to file them because I was going abroad."

His expression changed, softened. "I haven't been back to the vineyard. I came straight here from Vegas."

That would explain the more than twelve hour flight. She rubbed her eyes again. Was this really happening or was this all a dream? If it was a dream, she wasn't sure she wanted to wake up. Even if he was angry with her, he was here. And he hadn't deserted her. He had tried to contact her. He'd planned to come back for her.

Maybe she shouldn't have ditched her cell phone when she left the States.

No, she couldn't think that way. She'd done them both a favour by taking off. They would have ended sooner or later anyway, and the abruptness of his departure had saved her from a fate worse than death.

Except he hadn't filed the papers. She bit her lip. "So that means we're still married."

"It would appear so." He smiled grimly.

She had no idea if he was pleased by the idea or not.

She shouldn't be, but she was. She hadn't known until this moment, when the joy surged through her, how much she'd missed him. It wasn't only the chemistry she'd missed, though there was that too.

The chemistry was particularly hard to ignore right now, there was so much of it zipping around the neat little kitchen.

But of course it was stupid to hope. After her lack of trust in him and the way she'd run out on him so quickly, surely he wouldn't still want to stay married to her?

"Well now that we're both here, I suppose we could get divorced here in Westerwald?" she suggested tentatively.

"Not going to happen." His eyes weren't just hard. They were cold, blue steel. "Whether you like it or not, there is no way you and I are getting divorced. Not now and not in this country."

He'd said there hadn't been a divorce in his family in over three hundred years. A strange suspicion formed itself in her mind. "Is divorce illegal in Westerwald?"

He laughed, but it had a bitter sound. "You should read the newspapers sometime. Or are you that self-centred that you don't give a damn about anything that happens in the world around you?"

Ouch. Well, she couldn't say she hadn't earned it. She lifted her chin. "Care to enlighten me?"

"I hoped by now you'd have remembered."

There it was again. That black hole where her memories should have been.

Thanks to Google she now knew more than anyone needed to know about amnesia. She also knew that certain drugs, like the sedative she'd been prescribed, had amnesiac qualities. Nice of the doctor to fill her in on the potential side effects. Or maybe he had. In the wake of her father's death she'd been too wrapped up in packing up their lives and sorting practicalities to pay much attention. Her father's affairs had been a mess, which hadn't come as much of a surprise.

But all the knowledge in the world didn't mean a thing. She still had no memory of the day they met. Still couldn't remember her own wedding. How sad was that?

Frustration boiled over. "Do you think I haven't tried? I don't remember! I even went to see a hypnotist in Paris. It didn't work. I still have no idea what possessed me to marry you."

He grinned and for a second she glimpsed the old Max she'd known and loved before the grim, hard exterior reasserted itself.

She shook her head. There was no point in hanging on to anger. She needed to move on. "So if we can't get divorced, what do we do now?"

"Are you going to stick around a while this time?"

She met his gaze head on and unflinching. "That depends."

He arched an eyebrow. "On what?"

On whether she could resist the temptation to be seduced by him all over again. Even this new, harder, meaner Max was making her pulse jump more erratically than a rock star on speed.

She sighed. "It's late and I'm too tired for games. Tell me what you want from me."

He stepped close, so close she had to look up to meet his gaze. He placed a hand on the counter top on either side of her, hemming her in. "I want the same things I always wanted."

She sucked in a deep breath. His eyes flashed fire, but it was no longer anger that burned him up. Her body responded, with a yearning so strong she had absolutely no say in the matter. Seems when it came to Max, she never had any say in the matter. Her hormones led her all the way.

She lifted her face to his, ready when his mouth crushed down on hers, and met his hunger with a matching hunger of her own.

She'd craved this for so long. He tasted as good as she remembered, and his touch was still as compelling. He lifted her up onto the counter, and she wrapped her legs around him, pulling him as close as two bodies could get fully clothed.

He slid his hands into her hair, angling her head. His tongue penetrated deeper, and she moaned. She'd never wanted anything in her life as much as she wanted this man. Craved him, like a junkie craved drugs.

Her body throbbed with unmet desire. She grew wet in the juncture of her thighs. Her hands moved beneath the soft fabric of his t-shirt, sliding over skin stretched taut over hard muscle, her nails raking his skin.

Max broke their kiss and gently pulled away. His eyes were clear again, the hardness almost gone. He held her gaze for a long moment, and then brushed his thumb over her bruised lips.

"It seems you want the same thing I do."

She cast a glance around the compact, clinical kitchen. She still hadn't finished emptying the dishwasher or made the fresh lemonade for tomorrow. To hell with it. She'd worry about it in the morning. "Your place or mine?"

Max scooped Phoenix off the counter and set her back on her feet. He couldn't exactly take her back into the castle the way he'd come. Talk about a passion killer. And there was no way he was going to walk her in through the main gate at this hour, or her name would be all over the papers before breakfast.

But if she was booked into one of the town's guest lodges or bed and breakfasts…also not an option.

He felt like a horny teenager all over again. The one difference was that the French academy where he'd studied had been a whole lot easier to break into unnoticed than a fortified medieval castle that had withstood many sieges. "Where are you staying?"

"In a little apartment that belongs to Rebekah's husband. It's built right into the town wall."

Max knew the place. "Definitely your place."

He waited in the kitchen while Phoenix locked the café's front door, then he followed her out the back door into a narrow alley.

The massive stone walls of the town had once been the castle's outermost line of defence, and the wide battlemented walkway above was still popular with the tourists. These days the town sprawled beyond the walls and down to the river, but within the encircling walls lay the oldest part of town, cobbled streets that remained relatively free of traffic, with tiny shops and offices below street level and narrow passages that ended in surprising courtyards.

Claus's apartment lay at the end of one of those narrow passages. The courtyard was mercifully dark, lit only by the waxing moon. He climbed the rickety wooden staircase behind her, to the first floor apartment that was built right into the town wall.

The apartment was even smaller than her Vegas motel suite. A single room dominated by an enormous and sturdy-looking wooden bed – he grinned at that – an old-fashioned dresser, a kitchenette area separated from the rest of the room by a pale linen drape and a single door that he presumed led to a bathroom.

He closed the door behind them and for a moment they both stood, awkward and aware of the silence humming between them.

She pulled out her hair band and shook her shoulder-length hair loose. Beneath the bright electric light, he noticed that her hair was streaked with a subtle mix of red and blonde highlights, and it had grown out since he'd last seen her. With her shoulders thrown back, and the tight jeans and fitted tee, she looked more than ever like some young rock groupie. Streetwise, savvy, and yet somehow brittle beneath the attitude.

Phoenix cleared her throat. "Can I get you some coffee? Or wine?"

He closed the space between them, catching her in his arms. "The only thing I want is you." He said it like a prayer.

Then he lowered his head and kissed her. It was a slow burn, a volcano building inside him. The kiss that started gentle grew wild and fevered. Her arms wrapped around his waist, clinging to him and the blood thundered in his veins.

He'd dreamed of kissing her like this every night for the last two months.

He slid his hands over the smooth, soft skin beneath her shirt, lifting it up. He broke the kiss only long enough to rip the shirt over her head. She wore a bra of scarlet lace, skimpy enough that he could appreciate that her shoulders were now more tanned than he remembered, with strappy bikini tan lines. Tan lines she'd gotten on some Spanish beach, while she'd been partying it up without him, no doubt.

A dark, feral emotion gripped him. She was his wife. And he intended to remind her of it in the best way possible.

He stepped her backwards, then onto her back on the bed and she gasped as he knelt over her, his erection pressing hard and insistent against her thigh. He stripped off his shirt, caught the sharp intake of breath she couldn't hide and smiled.

He didn't bother with niceties and he didn't bother taking it slow. He peeled off her jeans and slid his fingers into the crotch of her matching lace panties. She writhed against him and he grinned when he saw she was as desperate for this as he was.

He moved the lace aside and bent his head down, intending to let her feel just a little of the torment she'd put him through these two months.

When her breath came in short gasps, her skin flushed all over, and she was within moments of finding her release, he withdrew. She cried out in frustration and struggled up on her elbows.

"Tell me you missed me," he said.

"Of course I did." Her eyes were wide and guileless.

"Tell me you were a fool to leave without waiting for me. You were a fool to doubt me."

"I was a fool. Now get inside me."

He grinned, victory tasting as honeyed in his mouth as she had. He stripped off his jeans and boxers and joined her on the bed. As he moved inside her, her tight, hot flesh encased him and he let go of the last of his anger and frustration in the sheer joy of coming home.

Her eyes fluttered open as he stroked a hand over her hair.

"Don't let me sleep," she mumbled.

"Why not? You said you were tired."

"I'm afraid that if I wake, I'm going to find out this was all a dream. Or worse, that I'll wake up with no memory of today."

He pressed a kiss to her forehead. "We haven't had a drop of champagne. And I'm not a dream. I'm here and everything's going to be alright."

She'd made him a believer. Any doubts he'd had about their destiny, about the possibility of Happy Ever Afters, was banished now she was back in his arms. He didn't feel old or alone anymore. He felt like a man who could do anything and be anything.

"I need some coffee." Phoenix slipped out of bed, with a flash of a smile for him. "*Now* can I get you anything?"

"Wine would be good."

While she moved to the kitchenette to set the kettle on and open a bottle, he sat up against the heavy wooden headboard to watch her. She returned with a steaming mug and a glass of dark red wine for him. He breathed in the bouquet and took a sip. "Pinot noir. Local."

"You can tell all that from one sip?"

He patted the bed beside him and Phoenix perched warily, like a deer poised to run. He suppressed a smile. She'd never been good with morning afters, but this one was a vast improvement over that first morning.

He glanced towards the window that overlooked the town and the river. The moon had started to set and dawn wouldn't be far behind. He wouldn't be able to stay much longer.

But he wasn't yet ready to leave.

"Tell me what you've been doing since you arrived in Madrid."

Her eyes widened. "How did you know I was in Madrid?"

Shit. He thought quickly. "I tried to find you. I called everyone who knew you. I spoke to your boss, your landlady, your friends." Which was all true, though none of them would tell him a thing. *Could* tell him a thing, it had seemed.

She glowered. "Khara should have kept her mouth shut."

He breathed a mental sigh of relief. Khara had some discretion, at least. Just as well, considering her brother had helped him procure the wedding license and might be able to put face and name together.

Phoenix looked down at the hands laced in her lap. "I'm sorry. I haven't thanked you yet for the money."

"If I'd known you were going to use it to run away from me, I wouldn't have left it." He reached out a hand and laid it over hers. "Was our marriage so bad that you couldn't wait to get away?"

She looked up quickly, her dark eyes wide and luminous. "Of course not. You were…" She swallowed whatever she'd been about to say. "I was ready to settle down with you and become a farmer's wife, for heaven's sake. It was as if I saw my life flash before my eyes: the SUV, the 2.4 children, the dog, and the white picket fence. I should thank you for leaving. You saved me from my own stupidity. I came so close to giving up everything for you, even my dreams."

"My pleasure." His dry tone couldn't have been more apparent. He hoped his pain was less so. She didn't love him as much as he loved her. She hadn't loved him enough to want to share her dreams with him.

She'd run away without giving him a chance, because she'd seen life with him as dull and stifling. How much worse would it be now, when she discovered that the life he could have offered her before, a life of ease in which they could have done anything they wanted, gone anywhere they wanted, was no longer possible? He was tied to Westerwald now. He had duties here, responsibilities. All those dull, stifling things she avoided.

He had no doubt she'd run again. What could he possibly do or say to change her mind? Whatever it was, he had to figure it out, and quickly.

"Tell me about Spain." He leaned back against the headboard and took a gulp of wine. The taste was raw and a bit too young. He made a mental note to schedule a meeting with the cellar master.

Her face lit up. "It was beautiful. The cathedrals, the art, the music."

He'd wanted to take her there himself, show her places he'd visited and loved, and explore new places with her. Instead, she'd done it alone. His jaw tightened. It cost him a great deal of effort to keep his voice light. "Have you been there all this time?"

"Oh no. From Spain I travelled through France, and spent a few weeks in Paris." She relaxed as she talked. Unconsciously, she leaned against the headboard beside him. They sat and talked, just as they had in Vegas.

She told him of her adventures, of the things she'd seen, and they shared reminiscences of Paris. His glass slowly emptied.

She moved to re-fill it, but he stopped her. The government might be on hiatus but that didn't mean he was. He had a day scheduled full of meetings and couldn't afford a muddled head.

Phoenix sank back against the headboard beside him. "You've let me ramble on. Tell me what you've been up to. Have you been here in Westerwald all this time since you left?"

She still had no clue, but that couldn't last forever. In a town infected with coronation fever it would be only a matter of time before she discovered the truth. But tonight he wanted to keep things as they'd been, pure and simple. Uncomplicated.

It was selfish, but he hadn't had a day free of complications since he'd left Vegas, and he craved it now. And perhaps if he could remind her how much fun they'd had together…how right they were together.

"Remember I told you my brother Rik was destined to take over the family business? Well something happened, and he had to go away." Max wasn't even sure exactly where his brother was now. Rik had stopped taking his calls. "So I had to step in and take over."

She frowned. "That's not fair, is it? You had your own life."

"We also had responsibilities, people who relied on us." He shrugged. "I've made my peace with it." He intertwined his fingers with hers. "There's only one thing I haven't made peace with and that was losing you."

She swallowed, looking down at their hands. "I missed you too. I didn't tell you that just to get laid."

"Will you promise me you won't disappear in the next twenty four hours?"

She nodded. "I think I can manage that."

"There's something we need to talk about. What time do you get off work tomorrow?"

"You mean today?" She grinned. "Same time, same place."

"I'll meet you back here at midnight, then."

"You're leaving?" The wary look was back in her eyes. He was learning to recognise it. He should have known she'd bolt the moment he left Vegas. For a full week she'd shied away from him, as if she'd been too scared to let him close.

The only time she hadn't been on edge, as if about to make a run for it, had been the day they met. That relaxed, easy-going

89

Phoenix had to be in there somewhere, under all those layers of skittish, hard-edged cynicism. Beneath the fear.

This time he wasn't going to give her the opportunity to run. The last two months without her had been unbearable. He'd known loneliness before and it didn't scare him, but living with her, though it had only been one week, had changed him. Living without her was a torture he didn't intend to inflict on himself ever again.

And soon Phoenix would realise that too. Destiny had brought them together again – and who could deny destiny?

"I have an early meeting, but I'll be back. Will you trust me this time?"

She grinned. "I'll give it a try."

He brushed a kiss over her lips, a cursory touch that was more promise than passion, and swung his legs off the bed. He had to hurry if he was going to get back in through the pantry window before the kitchen staff showed up for work.

He paused in the doorway. "Don't go flashing that ring of yours around. It might get you into trouble." He paused. "It might get us both into trouble."

What the hell did that mean? It had almost sounded like a threat.

As soon as the door shut behind him, Phoenix rolled over and buried her face in the pillows. His scent lingered on the pillow and she breathed it in. Tonight had been better than any dream. And for the first time in as long as she could remember, sleep overcame her with no trouble at all.

The little café was doing a roaring business. Phoenix hustled between the tables, taking orders, chatting to the customers, ringing up bills, while Rebekah presided over the ice cream counter. In this summer heat wave the home-made, family-recipe ice cream was their biggest seller.

It was late by the time business finally slowed enough for them to put up their feet and tally up the day's earnings.

"I don't know when I last felt this tired." Rebekah flipped the sign on the door (which said 'closed' in four different languages) and sat at one of the tables outside the café. The cool breeze outdoors came as a relief after the stifling heat of the café.

It was dark already and the town square was packed with people. A live band played at the pub across the square, eighties hits spilling out into the brightly lit square.

Phoenix set down two icy beers on the table and took a seat beside her. Rebekah sighed in satisfaction as she sipped her beer. "Coronations evidently make for good business. I've never seen the town this full, even for the annual music festival in September. Now all we need is for Maximilian to find his one true love and marry, and we'll be able to beat the recession blues once and for all."

What was with the people of this country? Did they all believe in fate and true love? Next, there'd be fairy godmothers and flying carpets. "Who's Maximilian?"

"Our soon to be Archduke." Rebekah eyed her over the rim of her beer bottle. "You've been smiling all day. What gives?"

"Can't a girl just be happy?" Phoenix grinned. Rebekah was right, she couldn't stop smiling.

"That's not just happy. That's an '*I got laid last night*' look. So who's the lucky guy and where did you meet?" Rebekah propped her feet up on an empty chair. "And where do you even get the energy to go out picking up guys with the hours I've been working you this week?"

Phoenix rocked back on her chair. "Actually I think he did the picking up. I don't remember. We met in Vegas a few months ago... That night's a bit of a blur." To say the least.

"He's American?" Rebekah sighed. "Isn't that typical! You travel half way around the world to meet someone from back home."

Phoenix wasn't sure why she didn't correct her. Perhaps because she wanted to keep Max to herself a little longer. Her dirty little secret.

"He's only half American and he's the real reason I'm here. I'd never heard of Westerwald until I met him."

"Not surprising. Aside from wine and fairy tales, we're not known for much. But there's nowhere else in the world I'd rather be."

"Have you never wanted to see more of the world?"

Rebekah smiled. "I've travelled. We are right in the heart of Europe, after all. But why would I want to live anywhere else? This is home. It's part of who I am."

Phoenix had never been in one place long enough for it to become a part of her. She wondered how that would feel. *Home.* For her, home had never been a place, it had been people. Or rather a person, until her father died, casting her adrift.

Then she'd met Max. That week he'd lived in her little apartment, she'd lost that sense of rootlessness. Perhaps that was why she'd married him. A way to get over her grief.

She swigged from the bottle of beer, and screwed up her eyes as a memory forced its way up to the surface. "My…" What was he? She could hardly call him her husband, even though it was true. Lover might be more accurate, but she didn't want Rebekah getting the wrong impression of her. She started again. "My boyfriend told me a tale I've been thinking a lot about lately."

"Oh?"

"About a ruler who got divorced and caused such a scandal that he started a war."

"That would have been Archduke Willem back in the late 1600s. He was beheaded right here in this town square."

"The story's real?"

"Of course. Aren't all the best stories real? Every school child in Westerwald learns about the civil war. But the part of the story I always loved the most was how a beautiful sorceress cast a magic spell on the royal family when the war was over. From that time on every member of the family would be destined to find true love with the one they marry, and live happily ever after."

It might as well be fairy godmothers and flying carpets. Phoenix rolled her eyes. "They didn't seriously teach you that in school?"

Rebekah shrugged. "Maybe not, but it's still fact. There hasn't been a divorce in the royal family in over three hundred years."

A chill shivered down Phoenix's spine. Max was a common enough name. Probably as common here as Michael or Christopher were back home. And there must be more than one family in Westerwald that hadn't had a divorce in centuries, because it couldn't possibly be *her* Max.

Besides, Archdukes were old men, not gorgeous hunks. And Princes didn't go around seducing waitresses. Even if they did, they sure as hell didn't marry them.

She shivered again.

"Are you cold?"

Phoenix shook her head. The evening had turned into one of those gorgeous summer nights, with stars bright in the clear sky, and the air balmy. Not as sweltering hot as Vegas, or muggy like LA, but perfect. Westerwald really was a fairy tale kingdom.

"If you want, I'll close up here tonight and you can go home to your husband."

"No point going home early. There's a reception dinner for the tourism council at the castle tonight that Max is hosting, so Claus is working late."

Phoenix shook off that odd feeling. "You're on a first name basis with the Archduke?"

"We were at school together as kids and I have a hard time

thinking of him as anything but Max. Claus says he prefers it, anyway. Apparently he hates all the bowing and scraping."

The chill down Phoenix's spine escalated into an avalanche. "I don't suppose you have a picture of him anywhere?" Her throat felt scratchy and choked.

"Sure, I must have." Rebekah swung her feet to the ground and headed back into the cafe. She emerged only moments later with a French tabloid magazine in her hands, flicking through the pages.

Unable to breathe, Phoenix took the magazine from Rebekah's outstretched hands. She let out the breath she'd been holding. "Wow!"

Rebekah grinned. "He's quite a hunk, isn't he?"

If you think he looks good here, you should see him naked.

To cover the shake that had started in her hands, she set the magazine down and sat on them. She needed time to think. Hell, what she needed was more alcohol.

"Since your husband and my…" soon to be *dead* husband "… boyfriend are busy until late, I think you and I should go out partying. After all, it's a Friday night."

The pub across the square seemed to be doing a pretty good trade. And the music spilling out into the square was loud enough and fast enough to drown out the sudden, clambering thoughts that she wasn't yet ready to deal with.

Rebekah clapped her hands in delight. "Great idea. Let's have some fun!"

Chapter Seven

It was well past bewitching hour when Max made his escape through the pantry window. With the late night reception, the kitchen staff had worked late and he'd had to wait until they were finished cleaning up and the kitchen was empty.

He scraped his knee on the window ledge as he slid through. This was ridiculous. He was sneaking around to visit his own wife. She should be in his room and in his bed right now. Preferably naked.

Tonight he was going to lay all his cards on the table and tell her everything. Even the dirty linen and the stuff they'd managed to keep out of the papers. And he very much intended to use the upcoming referendum to blackmail her into staying in Westerwald, if that's what it took.

Let her think this was all a marriage of convenience. It wouldn't matter. His parents' marriage had been arranged and they'd been devoted to each other, the sordidness of his mother being pregnant with another man's child when they married aside.

As soon as he could be sure Phoenix wasn't going to do another runner, he would set up a meeting with Albert. If the coronation worked out as well as the tourism council believed it would, then the prospect of a royal wedding ought to make his cabinet's day.

Since it was Friday night and the streets were far more crowded than usual, he had to take a circuitous route to get to Phoenix's apartment.

In the little courtyard before her apartment, a teenage couple sat intertwined on a wooden bench half hidden by a draping vine. He grinned. Seems like love was in the air tonight.

Angry indie rock music pumped from Phoenix's apartment. He took the stairs two at a time to knock on her door. It was a long moment before she answered. While he waited, the couple on the bench below paid him no attention. He didn't blame them. When he was with Phoenix the rest of the world had a tendency to disappear too.

She opened the door and the music was instantly deafening. Then she leaned against the doorjamb, blocking his way, arms crossed over her chest. *Oh-oh.*

He cast a glance over his shoulder. "May I come in?"

"If I don't let you in, will you have me arrested, Your Highness?"
Shit.

He attempted levity. "Not unless you enjoy the idea of handcuffs." From the look on her face, humour clearly wasn't going to do it. "Or unless you want your neighbours asking questions."

She opened the door wider and stepped back. He crossed the threshold and shut the door behind him.

Phoenix kept her arms crossed over her chest and didn't budge. She clearly had no idea what it did to her cleavage. And the anger flashing in her deep, dark eyes got completely the opposite reaction going in him. She was even more beautiful when she was angry.

The music battered over them. He nodded to the MP3 player hooked up beside the bed. "We need to talk."

She moved to turn it down and he sat on the bed, beside an open suitcase with half its contents strewn across the duvet.

"You're leaving?"

Since there was no other place for her to sit, and she obviously wanted to keep her distance, she remained standing. "How about I talk and you shut up?"

He nodded.

"So the 'family business' is basically running the kingdom?"

He didn't answer.

She glared at him. "Okay, you can talk now."

"It's not a kingdom, it's a duchy."

If she had lasers in her eyes, he'd be toast.

"And since you effectively conned me into marriage and won't get a divorce, I am now the...Arch Duchess of Westerwald?"

"Officially, that'll only be after the coronation. Until then you're just a Princess."

Most women would have got a kick out of being a Princess. Not Phoenix. She pressed her lips together tightly. "And when exactly were you going to tell me this?"

"I did tell you. On our wedding night. Though I'd like to point out…"

She held up her hand. He shut up. Stunning as she was enraged, he didn't think a murder rap for killing the head of a European state would go down too well for her.

She began to pace. "Have you ever heard of a Princess called Phoenix?"

"It's not your real name." That earned him another glare.

He waited with all the patience he could muster as she continued her pacing. She needed to burn off a little of her anger, he realised. Perhaps wine would help. He held up the bottle he'd brought, a crisp white, a much finer vintage than the unfinished bottle he'd left in her tiny kitchenette the night before. "Do you want a glass?"

"On top of the five tequilas I've already had, that probably wouldn't be a good idea."

He could do with a shot himself. "Do you have any left?"

She stopped her pacing. "I'm sure the Rose and Dragon will be more than happy to serve you one."

His sense of humour failed. She'd been in the town pub all night? Doing tequila shots on a Friday night, with at least half the young men in the town? His chest pulled tight and his hands fisted. If any man had touched her, he'd kill them with his bare hands.

Enough with humouring her. It was time to take command. He rose. "Okay, it's your turn to sit and shut up, and let me talk."

She turned mutinous eyes on him, but he wasn't having any of it. Their gazes locked for a long heated moment and what passed between them wasn't all anger.

She gave in first and sat on the edge of the bed.

That was better.

"When I met you, I had no expectation whatsoever of becoming Archduke. I had a great life in California and I wanted you in it. My job has changed but nothing else has. I still want you in my life. I *need* you in my life."

"But it's not just a job, is it? It's a way of life. And I made it pretty clear from the beginning that I didn't want to be married."

"That's not how you felt the first day we met," he reminded her gently.

A storm raged in her eyes. "Stop saying that! That wasn't me. It was the medication."

"Of course it was you. It's not like you were on Rohypnol. You still had free will and you chose to marry me. And somewhere underneath all the attitude, I believe you'd make the same choice again, if you'd only give yourself half a chance."

"However I may or may not have felt when I married you, I definitely don't want to be married to the ruler of a country. I'll make a really lousy Princess. I'm way too selfish."

"I have a selfish streak too. I couldn't care less what kind of

Princess you are, as long as you're a good wife."

She arched an antagonistic eyebrow. "And what constitutes being a good wife?"

"Be my friend and my lover. Be honest with me. Exactly as you were the week we spent together in Vegas."

The flicker of her eyes as she looked away was barely perceptible. "Haven't you heard the phrase *what happens in Vegas, stays in Vegas*? Nothing that happened that week was real. It was a bit of fun and now the fun is over."

"It doesn't have to be. Look at this as another adventure."

She bit her lip. "So if it doesn't work out, I'm free to leave?"

That wasn't quite what he had in mind. "You won't want to leave." He had to keep faith in his family's legacy. He didn't believe in sorcery but there hadn't been an unhappy royal marriage in Westerwald since the seventeenth century, and that wasn't going to stop with him.

He sucked in a deep breath. "I know what I'm asking you is pretty big. I know you don't trust what's between us, and I'm asking you to take a leap of faith. You're going to need to learn to trust me."

"Why should I?"

He'd promised her the truth. Even if it killed him to admit it. "I wasn't raised to rule. Not the way Rik was. I've pretty much done whatever I wanted all my life and never applied myself to anything. I don't know that I can do this."

He'd never admitted it out loud. Not even to his mother in that emotional, turbulent encounter before she'd done what Rik had done, what Phoenix had done: turned tail and run.

"Then don't. Surely there's someone else who can take the job?"

He shook his head, breathing out slowly. Too many nights these last two months he'd lain in bed at night in a cold sweat wondering how long it would be before they found him out to be a fraud. Worse, that he'd make a terrible decision and fail the people of Westerwald.

"I'm the last of the line." He paused to make sure he had her attention. "But when I'm with you I feel like a better person. As if I can do anything. I need you by my side – at least until the coronation is over. I'm not only asking for me. I'm asking for all of Westerwald."

She frowned, confused.

"My family's name is mud right now. Since Rik has been proven to be illegitimate, everyone in the world now knows my mother was pregnant with another man's baby when she married my father. That their marriage was solid and happy for thirty five years no longer matters. The secrets and lies have done their damage." To more than just the nation. Those secrets had destroyed his faith and he still hadn't recovered. He doubted Rik had either, wherever he was. Their mother had known the DNA tests would be done. She'd known, and she'd done nothing to fore-warn any of them.

He pushed away the unwanted thoughts and played his last card. "There are a lot of people calling for the monarchy to be abolished."

She crossed her arms over her chest again. He was more easily able to resist the effect this time. These were serious matters and it was hard to get aroused with the weight heavy on his shoulders.

"That's a good thing, isn't it? If they get rid of the whole Archduke thing, you can go back to California and the life you want to live."

The temptation tore at him. If only he could walk away, go back to the States with Phoenix and pick up where they left off. It wasn't the first time the turmoil had raged inside him, but the battle had never been so hard fought.

After a long moment, he shook his head. "It doesn't work that way. My ancestors have ruled this region for nearly a thousand years. There is no way I'm going down in history as the Prince who lost it all. The monarchy will not fail. Not on my watch."

"So what does this have to do with me?"

"If I can get through the coronation and win the people to my side, then when the government re-opens in September and the republicans call for a referendum on the monarchy, they won't have a leg to stand on."

She set her hands on her hips. "I repeat: what does any of this have to do with me?"

"The press are all over me at the moment. One whiff of another scandal and there's a chance the referendum will go ahead. Getting a divorce would definitely constitute a scandal. However, dating a pretty girl will boost my image. It'll give the people hope and show them there's a future and not just a past. So I'm asking you not to file the papers. I'm asking you to stick around and be my girlfriend for a while."

She resumed her pacing and he understood she needed time to think. He left her to it, and moved to the kitchen to open the bottle of wine he'd brought, pouring a generous glass. He needed the alcohol, even if she didn't.

When he returned to the room, Phoenix stood at the window, looking down over the town to the river below. He could see it as a ribbon of silver even from here. She faced him. "Why me? If you want to avoid scandal, there are other women far better suited to playing your girlfriend. What if the paparazzi rake through my background? It's not as if I have the most lily white past."

"Because you're my *wife*. I don't want anyone else but you." He practically growled. Didn't she get that she was special? That there was no other woman for him? "Your past won't matter. Everyone will adore you."

"How do you figure that?"

"You make friends easily. One smile and every waiter who's

ever served you falls in love with you."

"What if the press find out about our marriage?"

A marriage was less scandalous than a divorce, but he knew that wasn't what she was asking. She was wondering how she'd be able to get out of the marriage once it went public. He sipped the wine, but it did nothing to remove the bitter taste from his mouth.

What had happened to the starry-eyed Phoenix who'd said 'yes' when he went down on his knees? Or had she been nothing more than a product of a bad mix of champagne and medication?

"They won't find out." He said it with a great deal more certainty than he felt, and it worked. She uncrossed her arms. He grinned at the sign of weakening.

"It's no wonder we don't have royalty in the US. It's so darned complicated."

The exhilarating rush of victory surged through him.

"I'll stay in Waldburg for a while, at least until your coronation. But…" She held up a hand, commanding his attention. "I have three conditions." She held up her index finger. "I want this marriage kept secret. Don't think you're going to keep me here by leaking the news to the media. I want you to promise you'll do everything in your power to keep it between us. I don't mind being your girlfriend but that's as far as it goes."

There went that plan, shot down in flames. "I promise."

Second finger. "I'm not moving into any palace and I'm not giving up my job. If … and only if … the truth leaks out and you need a convenient wife on hand, will I give up any of my freedom."

He frowned. That was not part of his plan but he'd live with it … for now. But he was definitely done with sneaking in and out the pantry window.

She raised a third finger. "The moment your coronation is over and your popularity is secured, I reserve the right to leave."

He would never force her to do anything against her will,

though the mere thought of losing her again choked him. Slowly, he nodded.

She smiled. "Then we can get a nice quiet divorce and you can find yourself a more suitable princess. I'm sure there'll be more than enough willing maidens to help you get over your heartbreak at being dumped."

Not bloody likely. "That won't be necessary. You won't want to leave." He set down his wine glass and crossed the room.

A smile lifted the corner of her mouth. "Still so cocky?"

"You bet." He swept the suitcase and its contents off the bed and tumbled her onto it. As his lips met hers, he felt her shiver in response. "And now we've agreed you're going to be around for a while, it's time we start on the adventure part of this arrangement."

The light through the window turned an ashen grey.

"So what's on your agenda today?" Phoenix ran light fingers down over Max's bare stomach.

"The usual. Meetings with business people who want me to do something for them. Meetings with politicians who want to stop me from doing things for other people. And meetings with officials to talk coronation plans."

"Sounds like fun. Not." She lay with her head on his chest, feeling the rise and fall of his breathing. Their legs were entangled and he stroked a hand through her hair.

"But this evening I'm going to meet the cellar master of a vineyard in the hills to talk wine. Why don't you come with me?"

"Go out in public? Tonight?" Phoenix sat up so quickly she nearly bumped her head on the overhead bookshelf. What had she agreed to? She wasn't ready for this.

"It's not that public. And I have a surprise for you I guarantee you'll enjoy."

"I'll have to ask Rebekah for the evening off. I don't think she'll

103

be too pleased. You won't believe how busy this town is getting."

"Text me as soon as you have her answer. Or I could stop by and ask her myself?"

"Don't you dare!"

The more tequila they'd drunk last night, the less veiled Rebekah's hints had become about meeting Phoenix's boyfriend. Phoenix had no idea how she was going to break this news to her.

She rolled to kneel astride Max. "And please make sure you keep your phone switched on for a change."

"I promise." He pulled her down to his chest and kissed her, thoroughly enough that she completely forgot there was something else she wanted to ask.

It was another half hour before either of them paid the least thought to the new day. Only when the grey dawn light spread across the bed, did Max reluctantly rise and start to dress.

"You're going to have to hurry if you don't want to be seen," she cautioned.

He buttoned up his shirt, and then bent down to kiss her. "If we were in the castle, I wouldn't have to sneak away every morning."

She shook her head. "If we were in the castle, *I'd* be the one doing the sneaking. And with all the staff and security you have up there, I can only imagine the gossip. Not a great way to avoid scandal."

"But what a sweet scandal that would be." He smiled. "You've never struck me as a woman who worries about what other people think."

"It's not *my* reputation I'm concerned about." She stretched languidly, and re-arranged the pillow beneath her head. "Now go. I need my beauty sleep!"

The door clicked behind him, and Phoenix chuckled softly as she burrowed back down into the duvet. She was dating a prince. Dad would have got a real kick out of that.

As for all the stuff she should have told him, like Scarlett O'Hara, she'd think about it tomorrow.

The early dawn had already begun to colour the sky a dusty pink. Nowhere near as spectacular as a Vegas sunset but just as awe-inspiring. Or maybe it was because he was in a mood to be inspired. He hadn't felt this relaxed and happy in months.

Max strode in through the main gatehouse, past the security booth where the guard gaped at him open-mouthed as he passed. In the inner courtyard Claus stood, dishing out fervent instructions to the group of men surrounding him. As he caught sight of Max he waved the men away and hurried over, relief written all over his face. "Where the hell have you been?"

"I went out for a walk."

"After midnight? Alone? And you're only getting back now? Are you insane? I have half the town out searching for you."

Max felt guilty and puzzled in equal measure. "Why on earth would you do that? I'm not under house arrest am I?"

Claus wiped a hand across his eyes. He looked tired and strained, Max realised. Probably the way *he'd* looked before he'd found Phoenix again.

"Your brother did a midnight runner on us. As soon as the guards picked you up on the external cameras, they thought it was happening again. And the cabinet will kill me if I let anything happen to you. We're under strict instructions to escort you wherever you go."

"Rik disappeared from here?" But of course he had. Their mother had come here after the funeral and Rik had come to talk with her ... and there was that unprotected pantry window...

Max smothered a smile. He'd keep his brother's secret a while longer. "You didn't seriously think I'd abandon my responsibilities, did you?"

Okay, he didn't really want the answer to that. Only a few short hours ago, he'd given it serious consideration. He faced Claus. "New ruler, new rule: I'm free to come and go as I please. Unescorted, if I choose. And if the cabinet don't like it, you send them to me. You're all going to have to learn to trust me."

Twice in one evening. He was getting good at this.

"And another thing. If I choose to go out clubbing at two in the morning, or throw wild parties, or hold orgies in the Great Hall, then I'm going to do that too, and no-one's going to stop me." Not that orgies were likely to endear him to the public, but damned if he was going to live in any way other than true to himself.

Claus laughed. "You always were the trouble maker when we were kids. Nice to know the old Max is still in there somewhere."

The thanks should all go to Phoenix. She was the one who'd brought him back to life. He'd been at serious risk of becoming old and boring before his time. Another reason why he needed her at his side if he was going to be any good at this Archduke gig.

Claus' eyes twinkled. "May I ask one favour?"

"Depends what it is."

"Don't forget to invite me when you decide to throw that wild party."

Max laughed. "It's a deal." Actually, that wasn't a bad idea … he'd think about it later. "Now if the fuss is over, I need a shower and breakfast before my meeting with the Archbishop to go through the schedule for the big day. Are you joining us?"

Claus nodded, falling into step beside him. "The car will be ready and waiting to take you down to the cathedral at eight."

Max paused mid-stride. "It's less than a mile. We're not seriously driving?"

"It's the most secure way to get you there."

"No-one has tried to assassinate or execute a member of this royal family in three centuries and Westerwald is hardly a breeding ground for terrorism. New rule number two: I'm not going to drive everywhere surrounded by armour-plated glass. I want the people of this country to see I'm as down to earth and human as the rest of them, and that I have the same problems and issues as anyone else."

Though he doubted most newlywed men had to beg their reluctant brides not to do another runner.

They entered the castle's inner yard, beneath the ancient iron portcullis that hadn't moved in several hundred years, where modern surveillance cameras and infrared detectors now did the job instead.

"And while we're at it, rule number three: We're going to clean up our act. This government does not need to waste precious tax money on carbon-burning fuel, and I'm going to set the example."

And just like that he had his answer. He could do this. Every doubt he'd had about his fitness to rule, or his willingness, was gone. There was no chance he was going to evade his responsibilities. All those things he and Rik had so often talked about, about bringing Westerwald into the 21st century, and about changing the world, that was all up to him now.

Claus laughed. "Albert is going to have an apoplexy. But I like it. I can already see the papers calling you the Green Prince."

It sure beat being known as the Runaway Prince.

"You look exhausted. Have you seriously been up all night searching for me?"

Claus nodded.

"Go catch a few hours' sleep before we leave. This castle has enough empty rooms for you to doss down in."

"Thanks, I will." Claus yawned and walked away, then checked himself and turned back. "And have you seriously been walking all night?"

Max grinned. "Would it be more believable if I said I spent the night with a woman?"

"Definitely more believable. I'm glad to see you haven't lost your touch. But, you know, you could simply send a car to bring her up here to the castle."

If only. He paused in the doorway and faced his friend. "About that ring... I looked into it and it's not the one we were looking for." And with that Max headed into the private apartments, past the sleepy guard and into the dark, voluminous Great Hall.

Chapter Eight

Phoenix glanced at her watch. Two minutes to six and Max's text had said he'd be here as soon as her shift ended at six. She removed her apron, primped her hair in the café's little restroom, and even added a touch of frosted pink lipstick to her lips.

What did one wear for a date with a prince? She'd wanted to ask Max last night but he'd managed to distract her very thoroughly, and she'd never got around to asking.

For a girl who barely owned a dress, it'd been a toss up between jeans and cargo pants. She'd gone with jeans. And her favourite Doc Martens. But she'd swapped her usual t-shirt for a traditional Westerwald peasant blouse, prettily edged with bright-coloured embroidery.

Sucking in a deep breath, she returned to the café. Her heart thumped against her ribs. It wasn't so much that she was nervous of being seen with Max, as much as seeing him again. Though it'd only been thirteen and a half hours since he'd left her bed–she'd counted every one of them–already she couldn't wait to see him again, so much that her body ached.

She moved to the front window of the shop. Saturdays were market days and stalls with bright-coloured awnings filled the square. Though some of the stallholders had begun to pack away their wares, the square still thrummed with activity. Buskers in traditional garb played for the tourists and a group of children fooled around in the fountain under the watchful eye of the two policemen who lounged beneath a tree savouring ice creams.

Another quick glance at her watch. Perhaps she should wait outside. That way Max wouldn't need to come inside looking for her. Perhaps a car would pull up discreetly at the kerb, she could jump in and no-one need be any wiser.

She waved to Rebekah, who was occupied behind the ice cream counter and darted out the front door just as the deafening roar of two motorbikes entered the square, the sound bouncing off the buildings.

Oh god. He couldn't have staged a bigger entrance if he'd tried.

Every head in the almost entirely pedestrian square turned as the two black and chrome Ducati cruisers pulled to a stop in front of the café. Max, because even under the jet black helmet the front rider was undoubtedly Max, parked the bike and slung a leg over. She sighed her relief. Jeans were clearly the order of the day. He wore black jeans and a long-sleeved black shirt that hung loose over his hips, with the sleeves rolled up to display strong golden fore-arms.

The sigh from Rebekah, now barely a few paces behind her in the doorway, was definitely not one of relief but of awe. Phoenix knew how she felt. Max was a truly breath-taking sight. And as he removed his helmet and shook out his hair, the collective gasp from every woman in the immediate vicinity was audible.

My husband, Phoenix thought. Though what she'd ever done to deserve such an honour, she had yet to figure out.

The man on the other bike was half a head shorter than Max, with a slight build, his fair hair a shade darker than Max's, visible as he removed his helmet. Rebekah pushed passed Phoenix and headed straight for him. They kissed, long enough to raise a few wolf whistles from their audience, before breaking apart.

Rebekah waved Phoenix over. "Come meet my husband. Claus, this is Phoenix, who I've told you so much about."

Phoenix stepped forward to shake Claus' hand, burningly aware of Max on the periphery of her vision, the dimples emerging in his cheeks as he watched her.

Claus grinned. "Then I guess these are for you." He held out the bike keys to Phoenix. She refused to look at Rebekah. She didn't need to. Even without looking, she knew her boss' jaw had dropped open.

"You'll need this too." Max was at her side, already lifting the helmet Claus had discarded and setting it on her head.

His fingers brushed her neck with deliberate intent as he moved to tie the strap beneath her chin. His eyes filled her vision, the laughter in their blue depths too much to resist. He'd done this deliberately, made sure that everyone in Waldburg would know before the day was out that the Prince was dating the new waitress from the café.

So much for keeping this quiet. So much for avoiding scandal.

"I'm going to kill you." She kept her voice low, but the tremor of laughter gave her away.

"You and what army?" he teased back.

Oh, that's right. Rub it in. He had a real army he could call on. Maybe not a particularly big or ferocious army, since its function was mostly ceremonial, but still.

With the helmet firmly secured, she looked at last at Rebekah. Claus had his arm around his wife's waist. She still looked stunned so Phoenix could hardly imagine how she'd looked a few minutes earlier.

"I'll see you tomorrow," she managed.

Rebekah nodded, mute.

Phoenix slung a leg over the Ducati Diavel, slotted in the key and revved the engine to life. The bike vibrated between her legs and she purred her own pleasure. It had been so long since she'd last ridden a bike, she'd almost forgotten what a pleasure it was.

"Alright?" Max asked.

She cast him a scornful look. "It's better than a dune buggy and I am so going to whip your ass."

He laughed a low, throaty chuckle that sent a completely different vibration through her. "Yeah, but I know this area intimately."

The way his voice caressed the last word sent a shockwave through her. Liquid heat pooled between her legs. Not here, not now, not in front of all these gawking people. Instead, she channelled all her energy into the motor between her legs, revving the engine and releasing the clutch. Max jumped back as she took off.

The bike could have been made for her, reacting instantly to her lightest touch. She circled the square slowly, though she hardly needed the caution. The milling crowd parted before her like the Red Sea. She glanced in the rear view mirror and saw Max furiously refastening his own helmet and hurrying to follow.

Beneath the shadowy arch in the town walls, into the wider streets of the newer part of town, Max chased her as she headed for the river and the winding road that ran alongside it. As they turned into the main highway, the wind whipped at her and she laughed in exhilaration.

Nothing else mattered except that she was out on the open road, with the wind in her face, the taste of freedom in her veins, and Max closing in behind.

They raced for several miles, dodging between the desultory early evening traffic, until Max began to slow, indicating for them to turn. They turned off onto a narrower road, lined by the ancient forest that gave Westerwald its name, up into the hills. The trees gradually fell away to reveal rows and rows of vines on either side.

Sunlight flowed over them, rich and golden, and the air smelled sweet and clean.

Fleetingly, Phoenix wondered if this was how their life in Napa might have been. Even more fleetingly, she wondered if there was any chance their life in Westerwald could be the same, or if this was purely a once-off.

They slowed their bikes as the road dipped and curved through the increasingly hilly landscape, until they reached a wrought iron gate over a dirt drive. Phoenix followed Max up the drive to the quaint A-framed farmhouse tucked into the hillside and they parked the bikes in the shade of an enormous elm.

A tour bus filled the car park, its group of chattering tourists climbing on board laden with bottles of wine.

For a long moment, Phoenix sat astride the bike and caught her breath before she switched off the engine and undid her helmet. Max was already at her side, the dimple in his cheek working overtime.

"Enough adventure for you?" he asked.

"It'll do," she answered, horrified she still sounded so breathless. "This bike is awesome. It has so much power. I'm amazed Claus allowed me to ride it. You must have been very persuasive."

"The bike isn't Claus's. It's yours."

She had a slight inkling now how Rebekah must have looked, as her mouth dropped open. "You bought this bike for me?"

"I wanted a new bike for myself and I figured if I got you one too, it'd be something we could do together."

Just like that he'd bought two brand new superbikes? Seems there were a lot more advantages to being royal than not having to do your own laundry.

"Thank you." And she thanked him in the best way possible, in a fiery, breathless kiss that flooded her with sensation and robbed her of thought. Thank heavens she was still seated astride the bike as she lost all ability to stand.

When they finally broke apart, Max laughing softly, he had to help her off the bike. He kept her hand firmly tucked in his as they passed the tour bus and approached the farmhouse. The thrill of a bike ride at speed, with the river and forest flashing by, had nothing on the thrill of holding his hand. All the tension of the day, of the hours spent away from him, melted away as they approached the farmhouse together and the front door opened to greet them. Behind them, the bus coughed to life and pulled out of the car park.

A few hours later the setting sun blurred the landscape with a gentle brush. Max swirled the wine in his glass and looked out over the terraced vineyards with a sense of satisfaction. This land was in his blood far more than any Californian vineyard could ever be and it had taken Phoenix to show him that. With her at his side, his life felt right again and his future clear.

While Phoenix chatted animatedly with the cellar master and his wife, charming both with her interest and enthusiasm, he lounged back in his chair and watched her. The setting sun highlighted the red glints in her hair, and caught the delicate planes of her face, her high cheek bones and pert nose.

"You're welcome to stay for dinner," the cellar master's wife offered, blushing shyly. She'd had no hesitation opening up to Phoenix, but with him she remained formal and nervous. He resisted the urge to sigh. That was the only thing he still missed about the States, the way everyone treated him as an equal. Everything else he could want in life was right here with him now.

He smiled at Phoenix as she looked to him, shook his head and rose. "We'd love to stay but I'm afraid we have an engagement elsewhere."

The cellar master walked them back to the car park, where he extended his hand to Max. "Thank you so much for your visit and for your faith in us. I'll be very happy to take on your experiment."

Max was only too happy to find a winery willing to take on his suggestion of introducing the Zinfandel grape variety to Westerwald. The soil and climate was perfect for it, and the local wine industry needed an injection of new blood. They also needed a higher international profile. Selling locally was all well and good, but Max's vision for his country's future was a great deal more ambitious.

"Farewell and thank you," Phoenix said, using the local dialect. She spoke naturally, without the halting slowness of someone sounding out practised words.

The cellar master thanked her back, beaming broadly, then left them alone.

Max wrapped his arms around her and pulled her close. "When did you start learning our language?"

She shrugged. "My father always said an ear for music helps with learning languages. I guess he was right. So what engagement do we have next?"

He lifted her chin to kiss her, and she shivered, in spite of the evening's sultry heat. "I'll give you a clue. It involves a long, slow seduction, and me getting you naked."

"Mmm. Sounds nice. Race you back to town?"

He shook his head. "We're not going back yet. You'll need to follow me."

They mounted the bikes and she followed, travelling at a more sedate pace now that the sun was gone. The forest loomed again on either side of the road, hemming them in and Phoenix lost all sense of direction before Max led her off the road and down a bumpy track between the trees.

Lights bloomed out of the darkness ahead and Phoenix sucked

in a breath as their destination came in sight. A small glade in the forest, with a stream bubbling through. On its broad flat bank a picnic blanket had been laid out, scattered with yellow rose petals, encircled by coloured lanterns and complete with picnic hamper and crystal wine glasses that caught the light.

"In between all those meetings today, how did you find time to set this up?" she asked as they walked hand in hand into the candlelit circle.

"Like that." He clicked his fingers. "Turns out all I had to do was tell Claus I wanted to surprise my girl, and it was done. One of the perks of being Archduke."

She'd once thought she could get used to having a man around the house who fixed tap washers and poured her baths. This was even better.

He poured the chilled white wine from the ice bucket and Phoenix took a long sip before lying back to look up at the stars.

"That's at least the third glass of wine we've had this evening. Are you sure you don't want some food first?" Max asked.

"I have a cast iron stomach. I don't get drunk easily."

He laughed. "Except on champagne."

"Except on champagne." She rolled up onto an elbow. "Did I tell you I have this devastating allergy to champagne on our wedding day?"

"You did."

"And still you let me drink it?"

"You're a big girl and quite capable of looking after yourself. Besides, the champagne was your idea. Amongst other things."

She frowned. What did that mean?

"Tell me about your day." He began to unpack the picnic things from the basket, and she was sure he was deliberately changing the subject. Her eyes narrowed, but she said nothing. Much as she appreciated it, since she hated being reminded of that momentous

116

memory loss, why didn't he simply tell her what had happened between them? What was it he still hoped she'd remember on her own?

She shrugged off the questions and lay back again to look up at the stars.

"It was a good day. We were busy all day and everyone is so excited about the coronation. It's all anyone talks about in the café." In truth, the day had dragged. She loved keeping busy, and being surrounded by people. The worst punishment she could think of was to spend a day alone with nothing to do.

Until she'd met Max, that was. Now, every moment she spent apart from him was a new form of torture, and being surrounded by people couldn't make up for the loss of him when he wasn't near.

Not that she'd admit it out loud, of course. It was a small step from 'I want to be with you every moment I can' to 'I can't live without you.' A small step with very big consequences.

She'd already witnessed first-hand how that kind of love could destroy. The way the cancer had eaten away at her father was nothing more than a physical embodiment of what had happened to his soul the day of her mother's accident.

On the surface, he'd stayed the same happy-go-lucky rocker he'd always been but the saying 'the lights are on but no-one's home' had often occurred to her. He'd been lost. Without her mother to direct him, he hadn't been able to find his focus. He'd given up on his dreams and his promising career had drifted into nothingness. He'd been like an autumn leaf, blowing about on the wind, drifting from one casual liaison to the next, one town to the next, one band to the next.

Her father had wasted away long before the cancer got him. And Phoenix was never going to let it happen to her. She was going to stay in charge of her own life, make her own decisions. She didn't plan to drift through life, never achieving half the things she'd set out to achieve. She was never going to love someone as her parents had loved each other. She was going to make every single one of her dreams come true, and no-one, not even Max, was going to stop her.

She sucked in a breath. This was too much heaviness for a beautiful summer night. Tonight was about romance and seduction, not memories or dreams. Neither past nor future had any place here tonight.

She nibbled on the canapés Max set out on a plate between them. "Tell me about *your* day."

"Everything I expected. A load of dull meetings. More problems and very few solutions."

"Well, you know what they say about all work and no play…"

"That's why I need you." He abandoned the picnic hamper to roll her into his strong, safe arms.

"Oh great, so I'm just your play thing?" She mock struggled against him. But they both knew her attempt was only half-hearted. It felt too good to be touched by him, to touch him. "I'm good for more than just fun and games you know? I may not have had a fancy education but I have a brain. Talk to me."

"Are you sure you want to hear about it?"

She giggled as his stubble brushed over her cheek. He nipped her earlobe.

"Stop trying to distract me!"

"Okay." He stopped teasing but didn't let her go. "The day started with a meeting with the archbishop to hammer out the coronation ceremony. Then there was a meeting to talk about our role in the European economy, then one on the labelling of cheeses. And finally, a meeting on how to keep our skilled young people from leaving for greener pastures. Bored yet?"

"Your pastures seem pretty green to me."

He laughed, but there was a hint of sadness in the sound.

"But Westerwald isn't much fun, is it? The youngsters who can get out do. They go to Paris or Frankfurt or London. Or like me, they head for the States. We're haemorrhaging our young people and not only do we have a skills shortage that's hampering our growth, but who's going to support the nation and pay taxes when they're all gone?"

"So make the place trendy."

"They already tried it, a generation ago. That was the reason my parents' marriage was arranged."

"I thought you said it was a love match?"

"It was once they actually met. But my father wanted to give Westerwald a hipper image by marrying a supermodel and my mother … well, I always thought it was the money and title that appealed to her. Now I'm not so sure. Perhaps she was on the rebound, or looking for a father for her child. Who knows? Whatever their intentions were, apparently they took one look at each other and they were smitten."

"Was that how it was for us?" She hadn't intended to say that out loud. Or to sound so wistful. She didn't want to be smitten.

"Pretty much." He caught her chin, and raised her face to his. "I could have sworn there were fireworks when I walked into that bar and saw you."

She giggled. "It was Vegas. Anything's possible."

"When you're with me, anything *is* possible."

His hand wandered down her thigh and she swatted it away playfully.

"No fun and games. We're trying to be serious now. Attracting young people, and all that, remember?"

"So as a young person, what do you advise we do to attract young people?"

She hardly needed to give it thought. "Adventure sports, night-clubs and pop concerts."

Max rolled his eyes.

"I'm being serious. Fairy tales and wine are all good but one is for the pre-teens, and the other is for the … mature. You need something in between."

"We are never going to be Ibiza. Apart from a couple of months in the summer, Westerwald doesn't have the weather for it."

"The occasional rave or visiting pop star doesn't require perfect weather."

"Oh great, next the press will remember how they used to call me the Rave Prince." Max sat up suddenly. "But that's a great idea!"

"Of course it is. What idea?"

"A concert. On the eve of the coronation. We'll have a free concert in the castle grounds. All I need to do is find a major headliner act available and willing to come to Waldburg at the drop of the hat."

Phoenix leaned up on her elbow. "I might be able to help you with that." She sucked in a deep breath. Max wasn't going to like this. "An ex of mine is a tour promoter."

He didn't like it. His expression turned thunderous. "Is this the same boyfriend who taught you to ride a bike?"

"Of course not. There was at least six years between the two." And at least six other boyfriends.

Clearly the subject of exes was the only one that hadn't come up that first day they'd known each other. It was good to know she still had some secrets.

Well, that and her arrest and conviction. She had no idea what Max, honourable as he was, would do if he ever found out about *that*. The fact she'd got away with little more than a record and a slap on the wrist wouldn't matter. Nor would it matter to the press or Max's government.

But as long as they didn't get serious, Max need never know.

His voice was dangerously even. "Exactly how many ex-boyfriends do you have?"

Not counting the lovers who'd never made it to 'boyfriend' status on her Facebook account? She screwed up her eyes. "I have no idea. I didn't keep count."

She ignored his fit of pique and pretended an interest in the food he'd removed from the hamper. It was a tempting spread: canapés, caviar on wafer-thin Melba toast, fresh fruit kebabs. She picked a long thin slice of pineapple off the plate and took a bite.

"There's no need to go all Neanderthal on me. I haven't had as many boyfriends as you've had girlfriends." As he opened his mouth, she held up a finger. "Don't even think of denying it. I Googled you."

It had taken her nearly an hour after she'd shut down the Google page before she'd stopped feeling as if she wanted to scratch out the eyes of every woman he'd ever been with. From not wanting to be married to him to contemplating raw violence had been quite a terrifying leap. But she was over it now. Or she would be. Real soon.

"Don't believe everything they write about me in the press. I was never serious about any of those women."

Which was no doubt why the press had shifted from calling him the Rave Prince to the Heartbreak Prince.

"I wasn't serious about any of my exes either. They were all nothing more than a bit of fun." And the moment they'd stopped being fun and wanted to get serious, her Facebook status defaulted to 'single'.

"Is that what I am to you: another bit of fun in a long parade of men?"

Her throat pulled tight. Max was different from any of the other men she'd known. He meant more to her. But for exactly that reason, she couldn't let him any closer to her heart than he'd already managed to get. She forced a laugh. "Of course. But

121

if you're going to keep glowering at me like that, I might have to reconsider how much fun you really are."

Her attempt at levity didn't lighten his mood much, but at least he stopped looking as if he wanted to commit murder.

"You're more than a bit of fun for me. You're my wife."

She pulled a face and sat up, moving beyond his reach. Why did he have to do that – go and spoil everything with his talk of marriage and commitment?

"Well I'm not a one man girl, so you need to get over yourself." She rose and brushed the grass off her jeans. "We both have to work tomorrow, so we should start heading back."

He grabbed at her, pulling her back down onto the blanket. "Not so fast. Think you can blow me off that easily?"

She glanced south, at the bulge in his jeans, and cocked an eyebrow at him.

He scowled but the amusement was back in his eyes. "Much though I love what you're thinking, this isn't the place. It might be private property, but one never knows when a group of over-eager campers or night hikers might stumble past."

"Whose private property?" she asked, diverted.

"Ours. This is the last remaining part of the medieval royal hunting grounds."

Ours. For a moment she thought of him and his family, then as he wove his fingers through hers, realisation struck. They'd married without a pre-nup. Half of everything Max owned was now hers. No wonder he didn't want a divorce. When all he'd had in the world was a job at his grandfather's vineyard, that half portion hadn't been a big issue. But now she was entitled to half of all Westerwald's royal properties and the stakes hadn't just gone up, they'd sky-rocketed.

It wasn't in her nature to be mercenary, but maybe on a champagne and sedative high she'd seen an opportunity and jumped.

Maybe she'd known what she was doing when she agreed to marry him after all.

"We're all alone in a forest, long after dark. Do you honestly think anyone is going to find us here?" she raised an eyebrow as she slid her palm over the front of his jeans. "Where's that risk taker I met in Vegas?"

Max groaned. "This is not a good idea."

"What are you afraid of?" she teased. And it was more than her words that did the teasing. Max sucked in a breath as she slid open the zipper on his jeans. "You're not playing fair."

"I know I'm not." She freed him from his jeans and bent down to take him in her mouth.

He groaned again, a lower, more primal sound. "Just to set the record straight," he gasped. "I'm not afraid of anything."

And right there she knew he was lying. There was one thing Max was afraid of: losing her. The knowledge hung over her, a cloud dampening the mood.

Not today. She wouldn't think of it today. She'd promised to stay until after the coronation. That was already practically a lifelong commitment in her world.

She shut out the thoughts and devoted herself to giving Max pleasure, to making sure they'd both have memories worth remembering when their time together was over.

When the picnic was done and the wine bottle empty, they packed up the hamper and blew out the flames in the lanterns. No point risking a forest fire and burning down half her marriage portion. She stifled a giggle.

"I have to go to work in the morning. We need to get back."

He grinned. "Your wish is my command, Princess."

She resisted the urge to wince at the title. Princesses were over-indulged women who spent their days lying around in palaces eating raspberries or shopping for designer clothes. It wasn't her.

As she mounted her bike again, the phone in her back pocket, forgotten all evening, buzzed loudly. Who on earth would call her now? Hardly anyone had this number. She glanced at the incoming text.

It was from Rebekah. *Don't go home. The press are camped outside the apartment.*

She swore.

"What is it?" Max hurried to her side. His concern shifted to glee as he read the text. "So now you come home with me."

"I smell a set-up." But she smiled.

He shrugged. "I'd love to take credit for planning that far ahead, but I tend to be more a 'take your chances where they come' guy. As long as I get you into a bed before I combust that bed could be in Timbuktu for all I care."

She laughed. "Okay. Since I don't seem to have any choice, lead on."

They fired up their engines, the roar of the bikes splitting the night-time stillness of the ancient forest. Her last thought, before she headed the bike towards Waldburg and concentrated on the road ahead, was that she seemed to have lost a lot of her freedom to choose lately. This being part of a couple thing was seriously limiting.

Chapter Nine

"Wow." Words failed her. Phoenix looked about the immaculate castle garage and let out a low whistle. "Is that what I think it is?"

Max glanced where she pointed and grinned. "A 1927 Rolls Royce Phantom. That was custom built for my great grandfather."

The Phantom rubbed shoulders with a 60s E-type jag and "Oh heaven … a Triumph Bonneville?" The classic motorcycle looked as good as new, its paintwork gleaming in the low light. Her father had wanted one when she was young. It was one of the many dreams he'd lost interest in along the way.

"I rebuilt that one myself during a summer vacation as a teenager."

So he was good at fixing more than taps and closet door handles. The man had more talents than an X-Factor contestant.

"Most of the vehicles were my late grandfather's. He was something of a collector."

They parked their bikes beside the Bonneville then passed through another set of infrared detectors and a plate glass security booth into the castle's outer bailey. It was like passing from one world into another; as if she'd stepped out of the 21st century straight back into the middle ages.

They walked hand in hand along a colonnaded walk that edged a vast, brightly-lit yard surrounded by high stone walls that were topped with walkways where uniformed sentries patrolled, then passed through an arch with a portcullis and yet more sentries into the castle's inner bailey.

This inner sanctum seemed to have more towers and courtyards than Disneyland.

"You grew up here?" Phoenix stared up at the impressive keep, built of grey stone and intimidating in both colour and size.

"The keep's purely ornamental these days. When we're not in residence, the armoury and art gallery inside are open to the public."

She had to swallow. This late night tour of the castle was going from unbelievable to surreal far too quickly.

Max pointed to the more modest building behind the keep. "That's where I grew up. The royal apartments were remodelled and modernised in the early 1800s and we've lived there ever since. Though these days this castle is more of a holiday home for us. Our official residence is the palace in Neustadt."

She shook her head, unable to understand how it must feel to have roots that went so deep; how Max said 'we' and 'us' for events that had happened centuries before he'd even been born.

The Great Hall was a double volume space with wood-panelled walls covered in faded tapestries. Someone had left the muted lights on and lit a fire in the grate. Though it was midsummer, Phoenix could appreciate why. She shivered.

"The walls are several feet thick and made of local stone. Great at keeping archer fire and cannon balls out but not so good at keeping the draughts out," Max explained.

The flickering firelight glinted off a display of armour, turning them into scarily life-like figures. "Another family member's collection?"

"Oh no, those are hand-me-downs. You can still see the dent in this one where Archduke Anton was struck on the head by a sword during a tournament. He was a champion jouster in his time. That helm saved his life."

After that, she stopped asking questions. It only made her feel like an ignorant tourist being guided through a museum. Which was exactly what she was.

Max led her up the grand staircase to his private rooms. The royal apartments came as something of a relief. They were nowhere near as grand as they sounded. The rooms were small, appearing even smaller due to the dark oak panelling and low ceilings ornately decorated with friezes depicting hunting scenes.

These rooms were decorated in what the magazines would probably label shabby chic. Phoenix just called it worn and for the first time since she and Max had ridden past the sentries into the outer yard, she felt at home.

The living rooms were arranged around a larger central area, which Max called the Solar. Radiating off it were the dining room, a TV lounge with the first intrusion of the 21st century, an enormous flat screen TV with surround sound speakers, Max's private study, and two circular stairwells leading to the suites above.

"There's no kitchen," she observed.

"Down in the basement. If you need anything, there's an internal number to dial. There's always someone on duty, though I prefer not to disturb them this late."

No kidding. 24 hour room service.

"It must have been a magical place to grow up." She sank down onto the sofa that was probably once a vivid scarlet, now more a dusky pink.

"I want my own children to grow up here too," Max said.

He wasn't looking at her, which was just as well. She couldn't suppress her shudder of horror. Babies terrified her. Probably because she'd never really been around any and everyone she'd ever met who'd had babies had been forced to sacrifice so much for them. When your husband was a musician and on tour half the year while you stayed home to look after children, the chances of your marriage surviving were nil. And that didn't even cover the more obvious sacrifices like sleep, looks and sanity.

Her parents had managed simply by schlepping her along wherever they went, but she didn't need a shrink to know her upbringing had been somewhat unconventional.

Max turned and grinned, dimples flashing. "Don't get too comfortable on that sofa. We're headed upstairs."

By the sensual lift of the corner of his mouth she could guess what was upstairs. She hoped the mattresses were soft. Otherwise she'd have no hope of feeling the pea and then someone was sure to send her home for being an imposter.

The narrow stairwell curved up to a small landing with two doors. Max led her through one of the doors into yet another sitting room, with French doors standing open onto a small wrought iron balcony. "You should fire your security guys for leaving the door open. Anyone could climb in here."

"You think so?" Max laughed softly as he led her out onto the balcony.

Phoenix gasped. She wasn't afraid of heights. There was only one thing she was afraid of and she still wore the ring around her neck as a talisman of that. But the drop below the balcony was breathcatching. Where the castle's stone walls ended, a sheer rock face took over. The castle quite literally perched on the edge of a cliff.

She leaned out over the railing, arms extended, and closed her eyes. The night breeze whipped about her, a warm caress over the bare skin of her arms. "It feels like flying."

She opened her eyes with a start as Max wrapped his arms around her waist and pulled her backwards. She could feel his escalated heartbeat through the fabric of his shirt, pounding against her back.

"I was perfectly safe," she objected, annoyed and flattered by his concern in equal measure.

"That railing is at least two hundred years old. You might be willing to risk your life, but I'm not."

"That might possibly be the most romantic thing you've said to me all day."

"Then I'd better correct that." He turned her in his arms and raised her chin. His eyes glittered in the moonlight as his mouth came down to crush hers, sweeping her away on a tidal wave of erotic sensation.

The wave carried them all the way to the bed, where she was far too distracted to give any thought to the softness of the mattress.

Phoenix woke slowly, drifting up through layers of sleep to an awareness of warm light caressing her bare skin and Max's presence reassuringly close at her back. The room smelled of flowers. She opened her eyes.

A vase of yellow roses stood on the nightstand beside the bed.

"Did you click your fingers again?" She rolled over to look at Max who sat propped up on a mountain of pillows, a book open in his lap. He'd changed into sweat pants and a t-shirt, and she missed the glorious view of his naked torso. Those defined abs made the mornings after something to look forward to.

He kissed the tip of her nose. "Good morning."

She sat up and rubbed her eyes. "What time is it? I need to get to work."

Max shook his head. "Not a good idea. Claus called to say there are reporters staked out all around the café."

She glared at him. "I am not a baby and I don't need to be cosseted. Besides, if the café is full of press people, Rebekah will need all the help she can get."

Max chuckled. "Okay. But do me a favour and at least stay for breakfast."

"Deal. And if I'm going to have to face cameras later, I'll need a shower too."

The building might be more ancient than she could comprehend but the shower was every bit as good as the one in the Mandarin Oriental. She closed her eyes and luxuriated in the pulsating spray, so absorbed in the myriad sensations cascading over her skin that she started when Max opened the door and joined her in the shower.

"The advantages of staying married to me keep adding up: no more laundry or buses, and you get to shower like this every day. Are you convinced yet?"

"It is rather nice having a shower big enough for two," she conceded.

He rubbed a soapy sponge over her shoulders, down her back, and over her stomach. The soap ran in rivulets down her skin. She leaned her head back against his shoulder and purred with delight as the sponge slipped between her thighs. She widened her legs and sagged against him as he continued to tease her with his hands. She was powerless to move, needing the support of his body to keep her standing.

When she came, it was in an avalanche of ecstasy, a ripple turning into another and another until her whole body spasmed with pleasure.

He caught her against him and held her until the last of the aftershocks died away. Then he lifted her in his arms and carried her back to the bed, oblivious of the puddles he left in their wake. He laid her down on the bed and climbed on top of her, nuzzling her neck.

"Don't move," he instructed.

"Where are you going?" She struggled up on her elbows, her body already crying out for more of him.

"I need to find protection. We used the last of mine last night."

She laid a hand on his arm to stop him. "We don't need it."

From the sudden hopeful light in his eyes, she realised he read a whole lot more into her words than she meant. He saw this as taking the next step towards commitment. She'd only meant that since she was on the pill they didn't have to worry about contraception.

But now wasn't the moment to set him right. She didn't want a serious talk. Her body needed him with a desperation bordering on madness. Again.

Max cradled Phoenix's head against his chest, as his heartbeat recovered and returned to its regular steady pattern. If it weren't for her insistence on going to work, they could spend all day like this. Sunday was his one day off and there was nothing he would rather do than spend it with her.

But she remained adamant. Something about not wanting special favours or to leave Rebekah in the lurch. Much though he admired the sentiments, he had to struggle against the urge to shake her. What normal woman chose working as a waitress over being a princess?

Phoenix was anything but normal, and that was why he loved her.

He stroked her hair. "You can't go to work wearing the same clothes as yesterday." He leaned across her to pick up the phone and dial the internal number, spoke in rapid local dialect to the housekeeper, then set the phone back in its cradle. "Your new clothes will be here by the time we finish breakfast."

"Have you bought the entire shop again?" she asked.

"No need. This time I know your size."

131

"You're a quick learner. You'll be an awesome Archduke if you keep that up."

"I'll be an awesome Archduke as long as I have you at my side."

She shrugged out of his grasp and rose from the bed, the sheet slipping away to reveal long tanned limbs. She didn't reach for her clothes but instead for the shirt he'd worn yesterday. She only turned back to him when she'd done up the buttons, by which time his body was already tight and erect. The shirt barely reached her thighs, leaving a great deal of smooth skin exposed. He didn't need to touch her to know how silken smooth those thighs felt beneath his hands.

She raised an eyebrow, fully aware of her effect on him. "You promised me breakfast," she chided gently.

With any luck he'd manage to draw breakfast out long enough to put an end to her talk of going to work at the café today.

He pulled on his sweatpants, not bothering with a shirt this time. Judging by the hungry flare of her eyes as her gaze stroked his chest, it was a wise move. He took her hand and led her down the spiral staircase to the ground floor.

"Isn't the dining room that way?" she asked, pausing on the first landing.

He shook his head and grinned. "I asked the staff to set up breakfast in the garden."

"I'm not exactly dressed for public scrutiny." She licked her lips."And neither are you."

He wrapped an arm around her and pulled her hard against him. "That almost sounds like you want to keep me to yourself."

"I'm just concerned for your reputation." But her gaze dipped, giving her away.

"Liar." He laughed softly and kissed her, only breaking the kiss when breathing made it imperative. "This garden is secluded enough to keep both our reputations intact." He slid his hand from the hollow of her back and down over the curve of her ass, pulling her against him. "No matter what we do there."

The door at the very bottom of the stairwell stood open, the summer breeze wafting in the rich fragrance before the garden itself became visible.

Phoenix gasped and let go his hand.

It was not a large garden, just a patch of neat lawn edged by colourful beds of fragrant herbs and bright flowers and encircled entirely by high walls of grey stone. The only entrance to this piece of paradise was the single door from the private apartments.

The servants had set up breakfast in the colonnaded cloister that ran along one side of the garden. No matter how hungry Phoenix professed to be, she took the time first to wander through the garden, pausing to rub a sprig of rosemary between her fingers, and to smell the yellow roses that grew up a stone colonnade, while Max watched, the pleasure in her joy of discovery unfurling inside him.

She belonged here.

"It's not just pretty," Phoenix said on a sigh, turning to him. "This garden smells like heaven."

"My grandmother lost her sight as she grew older, so my grandfather had this planted as a garden for the other senses. Listen."

Phoenix closed her eyes and listened. As attuned as he was to this place, he didn't need to close his eyes to hear the rustle of the long grasses that edged the cloistered walk, or the whisper of the breeze through the leaves of the ancient oak that shaded half the garden.

Instead, he watched Phoenix's face, noting the moment when she breathed out and the tension in her shoulders eased. Like a deer sniffing the air and not scenting danger, she lost a little of the wariness she wore around her like a cloak. When she turned back to him the usual hard edge in her dark eyes was also absent.

"Okay, I'll admit it. Motorbikes, secret gardens…this princess gig is very tempting."

But was it tempting enough? They might have crossed a threshold this morning, and she may have lost a little of her wariness but he wasn't yet sure enough of her.

He headed for the breakfast table and held out a chair. When she sat, he lifted the silver cloche from her plate. She licked her lips again, an unconscious gesture that pulled his body tight.

Once they'd eaten, omelettes flavoured with herbs from this very garden and the wild mushrooms that were a local delicacy, accompanied by fresh squeezed juice made from oranges from the greenhouses at his palace in Neustadt, Phoenix poured them thick coffee from the silver flask that had been a wedding gift to a long dead ancestor from the Tsarina of Russia. That last bit of trivia he kept to himself. He remembered all too well the glazed look in her eyes as she'd viewed the coats of armour in the Great Hall.

How they viewed time was still the biggest difference between them. No matter how far from Westerwald he lived, he felt rooted in the past; his life just a moment in a history stretching back a thousand years and stretching forward another thousand. Phoenix, on the other hand, was very definitely a here and now person. She lived in the moment and gave very little thought to either past or future.

She set down her empty coffee cup and rose to inspect the red leather box set to one side of the breakfast table, which Max had been doing his best to ignore. "What's in the box?"

"My homework."

"I thought you said the government was on vacation?"

"It is." He pulled a face. "But my prime minister still sees me as that wild, impetuous boy who earned the title of Rave Prince, and he thinks if he can just break me in and train me right, I'll be more pliable and biddable than Rik."

Phoenix laughed softly and opened the box. "I think he's in for a rude wake up call."

"Call it a reality check. I'm not a kid anymore and I'm way more stubborn than he realises." Max grinned. "Besides, I'll outlast him. Our legislation limits the prime minister to two terms. I'll still be here long after he's retired." He sipped down a last mouthful of sweet coffee. "That's why the monarchy still has a place in this day and age: I'm in this for the long haul. My job is to look at the long term. It's not about being re-elected, or about lining my pockets as quickly as I can, or making a name for myself."

Phoenix lifted a few of the folders from the box and flicked through them. "Looks like I'm not the only one who's going to be working all day." A newspaper clipping fell out of one of the folders and Phoenix bent to pick it up. She opened the folder to replace it, glancing at the handful of typed reports, each with a bunch of magazine or newspaper clippings attached. "What are these?"

He tried to grab the folder from her. "Albert's idea of a joke. They're portfolios of prospective brides."

She held the papers out of his reach. "What – you dial up Brides R Us and they send over a bunch of suitable candidates?"

"Something like that. Except the portfolios are compiled by our Intelligence Service. I really need to tell Albert I'm already married, before he gets his hopes up."

"Oh no you don't!" She glanced at the contents of the folder. He didn't need to look to know what she was seeing. A minor European princess with impeccable family connections, the heiress to a prominent English hotelier, an American blue blood whose face was recognisable from the tabloids. "Any of these women would make a far more suitable bride than a waitress from nowhere."

From the neutral tone of her voice, he had no idea what she was thinking. It wasn't like Phoenix to fish for compliments, so he only shrugged. "But you're the woman I chose to marry."

She removed the last report from the pile and scrutinised it. An A-list Hollywood actress famous for her romantic comedy roles. "You should fire your Intelligence Service."

"Oh?"

She pointed to a paragraph two thirds of the way down the page. "This supposed spiritual retreat in the Bahamas was actually a stint in rehab. And it was nowhere near the Caribbean."

"How do you know?"

"Because an ex-boyfriend of mine was there at the same time. In fact, she's a large part of the reason we broke up. Well, that and the drugs, of course."

Another ex-boyfriend. His hands fisted. Of course, she'd had a past. A woman like Phoenix didn't get to nearly thirty years old without having a few skeletons in her closet. But just the thought of her with another man made his blood boil. And the thought of another man cheating on her made him want to commit murder.

He whipped the folders from her hands and stuck them back in the box. "Enough of this. I'm already married, so it's all moot. Now unless you've changed your mind about going to work today, we're running out of time."

"Out of time for what?"

"For this." He pulled her down into his lap, and slid his fingers down her neck, flirting with the skin of her throat, to reach the first button of the shirt she wore. He undid the top button and his fingers moved to the next one, hovering above the cleft between her breasts. "Sod it," he said, "it's my shirt anyway." And with both hands he ripped the shirt, sending buttons flying.

"You could have just lifted it over my head," she pointed out, voice husky.

"That wouldn't have been nearly as satisfying." He dropped his mouth to her throat, and his tongue began to trail the same path his fingers had taken moments before.

Max hadn't lied about the press presence at the café, but a handful of reporters sticking cameras in her face and asking obvious questions were easy to ignore. Phoenix was far more concerned about the reception she'd get from her boss and colleagues. She held her head high as she made her way between the crowded tables, aware of the whispers and the heads turning her way. Rebekah was nowhere in sight and someone else served at the ice cream counter today, the teenager who helped Rebekah on weekends. Phoenix's stomach knotted as she pushed open the swing door into the kitchen.

"When were you going to tell me?" Rebekah set her hands on her hips and glared.

So this was how it felt. Phoenix squirmed beneath the glare, as the chef and his assistant ducked into the pantry and out of the crossfire.

Rebekah bit her lip, her face softening. "I blame myself. I should have known, shouldn't I? Half American, recently returned from the States… I could have put it together, if it wasn't so…"

"Improbable? Unlikely? Unnatural?" Phoenix supplied.

Rebekah frowned. "Don't be silly. As soon as I thought about it, of course it made sense. Max has always been a bit wild. He'd never be interested in some dull, stay-at-home type of woman like any of the Westerwald women who've chosen to stay. He needs a woman who'll challenge him."

Oh yay. So she was the challenge he'd mistaken for the love of his life. Phoenix sighed. "Max might need a woman who challenges him, but Westerwald needs an Arch Duchess." A brood mare to raise the next generation of Archdukes.

Rebekah's eyes lit up. "A royal wedding is just what we all need."

Phoenix rolled her eyes. Was everyone in Westerwald this focussed on fairy tale endings? "No wedding. You'll just have to be satisfied with a coronation."

Her friend's face fell. It would have been comical but Phoenix felt no desire to laugh. "I'm really sorry to disappoint you, but this isn't anything serious. It's just a little fun, another item on my Bucket List. Last month it was the Running of the Bulls in Pamplona, this month it's Be Seduced by Royalty and next month it'll be the Oktoberfest in Munich."

"That's still *two* months away."

"You know what I mean."

Rebekah crossed the kitchen and wrapped an arm around her shoulders in a loose hug. "Who says you can't have it all? This is a prosperous nation and money is no object for Max. As his wife, you could travel wherever you wanted."

But not whenever she wanted, and not with the same freedom she had now. "What if I wanted to sunbathe topless or get drunk or camp out on a beach somewhere? I'd have the paparazzi all over me, and the government ministers all over Max."

"Okay, I don't have an answer for that one. You're right. But couldn't you find it in your heart to love Max enough to forego topless tanning?"

Phoenix pretended to debate the issue, then shook her head. "Sorry, no." She ignored Rebekah's appalled expression and knocked on her chest. "Can't you hear? I'm the Tin Man. I have no heart."

Rebekah burst out laughing. Phoenix was glad someone thought it was a joke. But the truth was she couldn't afford to have a heart. She couldn't afford to let the moonlight and roses get to her. Because if she did...no, not going there.

The vision she saw every time she thought of loving someone was too horrid to contemplate. It was her father, prostrate across the coffin of the woman he'd loved so much that after her death he was never the same again. He'd tried so hard to be there for Phoenix, to love her, but he'd been only a shell of a man, drowning himself in whisky and loud music and a constant need to keep moving in order to keep the pain at bay. And Phoenix was very much her father's daughter, in many ways.

Rebekah let go of Phoenix's shoulder. "You and I are so different, I don't think I'll ever understand you. That all sounds like fun, but it's so empty and meaningless without someone special to share it with. I'd rather spend my whole life here in Waldburg with Claus than travel the world alone."

Phoenix shrugged. "And the thought of staying in one place too long gives me chills. I still have so many things I want to accomplish in this lifetime. I told you when I arrived, that I'd only be here a few weeks. Nothing's changed." She reached for the apron hanging beside the door. "Now which tables do you want me to cover today?"

"I think perhaps you'd better stay behind the till today."

Out of sight, right where she belonged. Phoenix nodded and headed into the café to take her place. It was a beautiful day, far too beautiful to waste on *what if*s and *why nots*. She'd take every day as it came, the way she always did, and leave tomorrow to take care of itself.

Chapter Ten

At the polite knock on the door of his study, Max looked up. Albert stood in the doorway. No doubt come to check Max had been a good boy and done his homework. Max suppressed a sigh and waved the man in. "I wasn't expecting you until tomorrow."

"There is something we need to discuss that couldn't wait."

"And you couldn't call?"

"This isn't the sort of thing we could discuss on the phone. You made the papers this morning."

"I seem to make the papers quite often these days. Was there anything in particular that caught your attention?"

"This." With a flourish, Albert set the morning paper down on the desk between them.

Max glanced at the lurid headline and the over-sized picture beneath it. A grainy picture taken through the window of a tour bus, of an indistinguishable couple entwined in a kiss. "That brought you haring up from Neustadt?"

"No, this did." Albert laid another picture beside it. This one was less grainy, a colour photograph in close up of Max and Phoenix as they headed towards the wine cellar, oblivious of the curious eyes of the tourists in the coach. "I managed to keep this one out of the papers."

Max frowned. "We're holding hands. So what?"

"This girl you're with is wearing the Waldburg ring around her neck."

Max arched an eyebrow. He might have been an outward picture of restraint, but inwardly he began to seethe. "The ring is mine and I'm free to give it to anyone I want."

"But in many people's eyes that is tantamount to an engagement!"

Max allowed himself a very real grin. "Yes, I thought so myself."

"You cannot possibly intend to marry this girl!"

"Woman," Max corrected. "Why not?"

"She is completely unsuitable. Did you not look at the folders I gave you?"

Max pulled the offending folders from the red box on his desk. "You mean these incomplete, poorly researched documents? You'd rather I marry a recovering drug addict?"

Albert's gaze narrowed. "How do you know that?"

"You might want to put a tabloid reporter or two on the Intelligence payroll."

"Be that as it may, you still cannot marry a girl you picked up in a Las Vegas motel."

The blood roared between Max's ears and it was only with great effort he remained seated. "You want to bet?"

Albert's face turned an unhealthy shade. He seemed to be doing that a lot lately. "Before you do anything rash, you should read this." He placed another folder on the desk between them.

Max picked it up and flipped through the pages. It was a long, long moment before he had his voice under sufficient control to speak again. "Let me make sure I understand you..." He spoke slowly and deliberately. "You had my girlfriend investigated, without my knowledge? On what grounds?"

Albert looked only slightly put out. "You asked me to look

for her. Besides, who you marry is a matter of national concern."

"No, who I marry is my own business. This is an invasion of my privacy. Our privacy." Max rose from the chair, drawing himself to his full height. "Who I date, who I sleep with or who I marry is of no concern to anyone but myself. Is that clear?"

"Would you bring Westerwald into disrepute?"

"This isn't the seventeenth century, Albert. It's not a crime to marry someone from the other side of the tracks."

"Are you aware her parents never married? That she never finished high school? Or that she has a conviction for possession of cannabis? Before you get too serious about this girl, perhaps you should find out more about her."

He didn't need to know anything more about Phoenix. He already knew everything that was important. Max rose from the chair, standing to his full height. "The same constitution that gives every citizen the right to privacy applies to me too. You want to change the laws? By all means try. I think your electorate will stand for it even less than I will."

Phoenix's soft laugh echoed in his head. It was time for that reality check. "If you think for one moment I'm going to be more malleable than my brother and you're going to control me, you'd better think again. I make my own decisions. Is that clear?"

Albert's eyes narrowed but he nodded. "Yes, Your Highness."

Max resumed his seat. "Now that you're here, I'd like to discuss a few ideas Phoenix had for encouraging our young people to stay in Westerwald."

Albert looked as if he'd sucked a particularly sour lemon. Swallowing his satisfaction, Max pulled out the notes he and Phoenix had put together in the early hours of the morning. If he could entice Phoenix to stay, then anything was possible.

Days blurred into one another, passing more quickly than

Phoenix could have imagined. By day she worked in the café, serving drinks to tourists who often came for the pleasure of gawking at her – or maybe hoping Max would drop by to visit her again but in that they were disappointed.

Much as she wanted to avoid the press, she couldn't. The wretched photographers were everywhere. She learned to ignore them, but every morning she flipped through the newspapers in the café, holding her breath until she was sure their secret was still safe.

Nothing else was, though. The press raked through her past and uncovered every sordid moment, including a few Facebook photos she'd be happy never to see again.

It was a relief when a fresh news story broke, something about a senior government official caught with a mistress in a Paris love nest. The journos lost interest in her and life in the café returned to normal. Or as normal as life could be in a town gripped by coronation fever.

It was the nights Phoenix lived for. Golden, summer evenings when she and Max explored the countryside on their bikes, visiting vineyards and racing along the country roads with the wind in their faces. Sometimes they picnicked in their tiny secluded garden, discussing the coronation plans or debating his nation's future. They chose menus for the gala dinner, wrote Max's coronation speech and laughed over a tabloid's speculation that Max had already broken the heart of his American waitress and moved on.

One evening Claus and Rebekah joined them for dinner, to discuss plans for the big concert. Rebekah squeed at the news of the band that would headline the show. "They were my favourite band growing up!"

"Mine too," Phoenix said, suppressing a smile.

"The lead singer, Johnny, is to die for, isn't he? I used to have his poster up on my wall, right above my bed."

Claus laughed indulgently at his wife's enthusiasm and turned to Phoenix. "I don't suppose you happen to have a convenient ex with connections in pyrotechnics? Because I could really use help with sorting the coronation fireworks display."

Phoenix ignored Max's dark expression. "Sorry, can't help you with that."

But the best part of every day were the hours they spent in bed, exploring one another, teasing, limbs entangled, hearts racing. Phoenix had never been so happy.

"This is how it can be forever." Max lifted the chain around her neck and cushioned the ring in his palm. "All you have to do is move this to your finger."

Phoenix turned her head away. "There's no such thing as forever."

On the morning of the concert, Phoenix woke to the sound of rain against the windows. She buried her head beneath the pillows, not wanting to know. So much for the land of fairy tale happy endings.

"It's ruined!" she wailed.

"No, it's not. The groundsmen will lay out ground covers to keep the yard from turning to mud and the weather will clear by evening," Max answered, unperturbed as ever.

"How can you be so sure?" She peeked out from beneath the pillow.

"Because I have a hotline to the met office. Don't worry. We've been doing this for centuries. That same yard used to be a tiltyard for jousting tournaments and people would come from all over Europe to attend. You don't think a spot of rain would bother the knights?"

She smacked him with the pillow. "Stop with the centuries thing already. I get it. Your family have a lot of history. Don't let it go to your head."

144

"That's why I need you, so you can keep cutting my ego down to size." He slid his arms around her waist and cushioned her against him.

"I don't!"

"Really? You keep telling me you can't wait to get away from me. How am I supposed to feel about that? It's a week to the coronation. Are you going to stay after that?"

She wasn't prepared to answer. She didn't have any answer he'd want to hear. She didn't even know if she'd make another week. She couldn't stay much longer without losing her heart. Already she was way more involved than she should be.

Any more involved could lead to disaster. What if the press found out some of her secrets? Max would never forgive her for lying to him. She knew better than anyone how his trust had been shaken, how he felt betrayed by those he loved. She couldn't bear to hurt him any more than he'd already been hurt, and every day longer she spent with him, the greater the risk grew that he would find her out. That he'd feel she'd betrayed him.

So she buried her head in his shoulder, breathing him in, saving up the memories to treasure later, when he was no longer around. "You'll get over it. You have enough confidence for three grown men." At least, she hoped so. He was going to need it. "I smell breakfast. Let's get up." She tried to leave the bed but Max pulled her back.

"Not so fast." He nuzzled her neck. "Not before I've had a chance to kiss you properly."

The bacon was barely warm by the time they reached the dining room where invisible servants had set out breakfast this morning. Grey light fell through the mullioned windows, turning the room murky, settling a gloom that the warm yellow lights of the overhead chandelier couldn't quite dispel.

Or perhaps it was because, in spite of Max's kisses, the thought of her imminent departure still insisted on intruding.

When he left, to greet the first of the visiting dignitaries to arrive for the coronation, Phoenix paced the Solar. Whenever Max wasn't around, the walls seemed to press in on her, like a cage. In spite of the discreet luxury, the royal apartments were exactly that — a cage. She couldn't go out without attracting attention. And with Rebekah's parents back in town for the coronation, and helping out in the café, she had nothing better to do than watch television.

Phoenix hardly ever watched television.

She leaned on the wrought-iron railing of the balcony and looked out over the terraced vineyards. The sky was leaden, pressing down, but at least the rain had stopped. A chill breeze teased at the fronds of her hair. She closed her eyes and breathed in the scent of wet earth, the scent of adventure and exhilaration, of everything she craved.

Well, nearly everything.

Somehow Max had wormed his way in at the top of the list of things she craved. There was no way she was going to be able to leave now without heartache. But she still had to do it. A little heartbreak now was better than a lifetime of pain later. She needed to get away, to say goodbye, before it became impossible.

But right now, she needed to get out of this apartment. Her bike and the freedom of the open road, called her.

Downstairs in the Great Hall, where a reception was to be held before the concert, the no longer invisible servants scurried around, polishing armour, scrubbing floors and setting up a bar at the far end of the hall beneath the minstrel gallery.

Phoenix wandered over to take a look. "Not like that," she said to the youth packing bottles onto the shelves behind the bar. She slid beneath the bar flap. "There's a skill to packing a bar so the barmen can find everything they need quickly."

And before she knew it, the bike ride was history and she

was stocking the bar, filling ice trays, cleaning glasses and slicing lemons, on a first name basis with half the servants working around her.

"You really shouldn't be doing this," the bar manager said, scrutinising her handiwork with approval.

"Nonsense. What else do I have to do? Get my nails done? No thanks." It was much better to be active. Sitting alone in the royal apartments was no fun. Being here, amongst the electric buzz as the castle geared up to open its doors to the public, was.

"There you are! I've been looking everywhere for you."

She turned to face Claus. "You found me."

"I have a job for you to do, if you'll follow me."

She smiled. A real purpose at last.

Claus led her to his office in an ante-chamber behind the hall. "Max will greet the guests as they arrive at the reception. In the past, his mother always stood by his father and helped him. Max will need you to do the same."

This was certainly the last thing she'd expected. "That's a really bad idea, Claus. People will think…" She couldn't bring herself to finish the sentence. She didn't need to. It was obvious what the world would think if she stood beside Max as his equal, as his partner.

"People already think. After all, you wear the Waldburg ring over your heart."

Her hand flew to the chain around her neck. "I can't!"

How could she explain to Claus that it wasn't what the rest of the nation thought that mattered? Max would think… he would hope.

Claus' level gaze met hers. "It's not that difficult. I've made some notes on the guests, and I'll coach you. They will be announced as they enter and all you need to do is say a few personal words to each person to make them feel special. It's a simple memory trick."

If only all memories were that simple. "Did Max put you up

147

to this?"

"He's already got a lot on his shoulders. I didn't want to burden him with this too."

When he put it like that, it was hard to refuse.

She and Claus were still bent over the guest list when Max returned. She felt the familiar pull in her stomach and looked up. He leaned in the doorway, arms crossed over his chest. He wore a pair of dark jeans slung low on his hips and a dark long-sleeved turtle neck shirt that clung to his torso, and her heart kicked up a beat at sight of him.

He pushed away from the doorjamb. "I can't leave you alone for a moment without you getting into mischief, can I?"

A guilty flush crept up Claus' neck as he looked from Max to Phoenix. "I was just preparing Phoenix for the meet and greet this evening." His eyes grew clouded. "I hope I haven't presumed too much?"

Max's self-satisfied smile showed how much he approved of Claus' presumption. And Phoenix's complaisance. She pushed the papers away and stood, her irritation levels rising. She had a score to settle with Max. But she managed to smile sweetly for Claus' benefit. "It was either work or run away."

If Max sensed the tension in her tone, he didn't show it. The dimple flashed in his cheek as he looked at Claus. "Then I owe you a huge debt of gratitude for keeping my...girlfriend...busy today."

Claus laughed. "She's a natural. You really should marry her, you know."

Max's amused gaze met and held Phoenix's. "Yes, I really should."

She frowned. "It's getting late. We need to get ready for the reception." She grabbed Max's arm and propelled him out the office and towards the back stairs the servants used to reach the royal apartments. As soon as they were out of earshot, she hissed,

"You didn't tell me the significance of this ring. Now everyone believes we're engaged."

"It doesn't matter what anyone thinks. I gave you that ring because you're my *wife*."

"That's easily remedied." She stalked off up the stairs, too angry to speak. If Max thought he was going to trap her here with a stupid ring, then he could think again. Because she was no Rapunzel to stay stuck in a tower.

Despite the fact that the stage had been set up on the far side of the castle, the thump of the warm-up act's music vibrated in the floor beneath Max's feet as he welcomed his guests. No-one else seemed to notice the discordant pulse beneath the babble of voices in the Great Hall but to Max it thrummed through him.

Beside him, Phoenix was all smiles, charming his guests with just a few words. She was a quick study, her memory for names and faces was excellent and wearing the same elegant teal cocktail dress he'd bought for her in Vegas, she was a knock-out. His guests loved her. She'd even won over Albert.

But beneath the bright smile and easy grace, something was wrong.

She might be at his side, as his partner, but he was losing her and he had no idea what more he could do to hold on to her.

The Hall was now filled with people, the concert organisers, local celebrities and the sons and daughters of Westerwald's rich and famous. And the headlining rock band too, clustered around the bar. Probably not the best place for performers about to go on stage.

With their duty at the door done, Max shepherded Phoenix through the crowd. He needed a drink and perhaps alcohol would take the edge off her restlessness.

"Would you like a drink?" He had to shout to be heard over

the din.

"Anything, as long as it doesn't have champagne in it."

He leaned on the bar counter and waved for the barman's attention. "Two margaritas."

One of the rock band peeled away from the bar and moved towards them. Max recognised him as the drummer.

"As I live and breathe, if it isn't Phoenix Montgomery! Hey, Johnny, look who's here," the drummer called over his shoulder to the band's lead singer, an icon and pin-up the world around. Johnny looked around and was instantly on his feet, moving to sweep Phoenix off her feet and wrap her in a tight hug. Max found himself shouldered aside.

She laughed. "Hey Mick, Johnny. I'm surprised you recognised me. I must have been about fifteen or sixteen last time I saw you."

Johnny grinned. "Fifteen. But look at you. All grown up and legal now." He set Phoenix down but kept an arm around her shoulder. Max forced his fists to unclench.

"How could we not know your face, luv? You're unforgettable," Mick chimed in.

It was the first time Max could remember seeing her blush. She also looked happier than he'd seen her all day. As if finally remembering him, she held out a hand to him. "Mick, Johnny, this is Max."

Johnny let go of Phoenix's waist to shake Max's hand and Max took the opportunity to insert himself into the space between them.

"My father toured with them one summer," she explained.

So she'd meant a whole lot more than posters on the wall when she said they were her favourite band.

"Time to get on stage, gentlemen." The man who interrupted wasn't a middle-aged rocker like the others. He was around Max's age, dark-haired and dark-eyed in that suave Latino way that girls swooned over. "Hello, Phoenix."

Not another bloody admirer. Phoenix had more groupies than the band, it seemed. Max wasn't used to having so much competition for any woman's attention. And he certainly wasn't willing to share Phoenix's attention. He wrapped a possessive arm around her waist.

"Hello, Rafael." Her tone was decidedly cooler than it had been with the band. So this then was the ex-boyfriend who'd put the concert together at such short notice.

Max smiled, but he kept a firm hold on his wife. "Thank you very much for helping us out."

The other man's eyes hadn't left Phoenix's face. "I'd do anything for Phoenix, and she knows it."

Max resisted the urge to growl. "Don't you have a concert to supervise?"

Rafael nodded, spared one last, lingering look for Phoenix, and turned on his heel to follow the band through the crowd that was dissipating fast as everyone hurried to their seats.

"Your drinks," said the barman, pushing the drinks across the counter towards them.

Phoenix ignored him to glare at Max. "What was that all about?"

"What?" he asked, aiming for innocent.

"That Neanderthal '*this is my woman*' thing you were doing?"

Anger spiked through his veins, so hard and fast that for a moment he lost all sense. "Because you are mine. You are not available. It seemed as if everyone needed to be reminded of that. You included."

"You don't own me, Max. If there's one thing I know about our marriage ceremony, it's that there's no way in hell I vowed to obey you."

She'd been insistent that night too. He drew in a deep breath and fought to get his own temper back under control.

Sparks shot from her eyes. "This was a mistake. It was a mistake back in May and it's still a mistake. No amount of time is going to make us more compatible or more suited to each other."

What the hell had brought this on? "We are perfectly compatible. Or do I need to remind you?" He lifted her chin, his intention to kiss her clear but she pulled away, taking a step back.

"In bed, yes. But in every other way we're completely different. You can trace your family back a thousand years. I never even met my grandparents. You have duties and responsibilities and I don't even own a goldfish."

"That's all superficial. We match in every way that counts."

"You need heirs, and I don't want children."

Her words fell like lead between them.

Okay, that was a biggie. He wanted a family with her. He wanted to give her the family she'd never had. Yet, she'd rejected it out of hand, without even knowing what she was losing out on. He swallowed against the hard lump in his throat.

This was starting to feel like a losing battle. What hope did he have of reaching her, when she'd spent so many years hardening her heart?

Even though he knew that beneath all those layers, beneath all the hardness, lay a passionate, vibrant heart full of love. He'd known it the first night they met, and he'd been trying to get back there for months, but it seemed he'd been attempting the impossible. Like her father, she'd turned running away into an art form.

She took another step back. Away from him. He felt the divide open between them, a gaping chasm that he had no idea how to cross.

"This is neither the time nor place. We can discuss this later. Right now, we have a few thousand people waiting for us to take our seats so the concert can start."

Phoenix downed her margarita and nodded. "Okay, I'm ready."

The acoustics in the outer bailey were incredible and the band was still as thrilling on stage as they'd been a decade earlier, but Phoenix found it impossible to focus on the concert. She longed for another margarita, anything to take the edge off her volatile emotions and taut nerves.

While Max appeared to have forgotten their tiff and seemed to be enjoying the show, she couldn't. She should have been happier. For weeks she'd helped plan this night and it was a phenomenal success.

Too phenomenal a success. It had been so easy to stand beside Max and to smile and greet the new arrivals at the reception. The same skills that had bought her years of free drinks from strangers in bars had Max's guests eating out of the palm of her hand. Even that stuffed-shirt prime minister had cracked a smile for her.

Who could have guessed that a lifetime of moving on, of having to make friends in every new town, would give her exactly the skills she'd need to be a princess?

But just because she could do the job, didn't mean she should.

Max would be far better off with a woman at his side who wouldn't bring him or his family into disrepute. If the press ever found out about her drug conviction, she couldn't even imagine the fall out in this conservative little country. And she never wanted Max to look at her the way he'd looked that night when he'd spoken of his mother's secrets. Angry, hurt, betrayed. She couldn't do that to him.

No, it was better for Max and it was better for her that they called this whole thing off before any of that got out.

He could sign those divorce papers waiting for him in California and she'd happily file them for him. Well, maybe not happily, but she'd do whatever had to be done to keep his reputation safe. And hopefully no-one would ever connect the 'Max Waldburg' on their marriage certificate to a foreign prince.

She heaved a sigh. She'd have to force him into it. She knew better than anyone that once Max was focussed on what he wanted, he was unstoppable. He always got what he wanted and he wouldn't let her go.

She'd have to leave when he least expected it, without saying goodbye, or he'd talk her out of it. And she wasn't placing any bets on her ability to withstand his persuasion.

The band moved into a ballad and in the yard below the royal box lighters sparked into action, a sea of tiny lights waving in time to the music. The words of the familiar love song wrapped around her. Moved by the music and the poignant lyrics, her heart ached.

Max wrapped his arms around her and leaned his chin on her shoulder and they swayed to the music. Phoenix closed her eyes, leaning back into him, drawing on his strength. But her mind was made up. She'd take this one last night with him, and tomorrow she'd pack her bags and slip away.

Her head might be on board with the plan, but her heart was an altogether different matter. It wasn't nearly so easy to convince and she didn't hold out much hope of keeping her heart as safe or undamaged as Max's reputation. All she could do now was prevent herself falling any further than she already had.

His heat filtered through the elegant tuxedo he wore, through the much thinner layer of her dress, suffusing her in a lust-filled haze. No. The 'L' word was no longer Lust.

It was Love.

She loved Max and she'd do anything for him. Including leaving him.

Chapter Eleven

Ignoring the 'Closed' sign on the café door, Max tried the handle. It turned and he pushed it open.

"We're not yet open." Rebekah poked her head around the kitchen door. "Oh, it's you. You look awful."

"Where is she?"

"Who?"

He scowled. "Don't mess with me, Rebekah. I've been to the apartment and I know she's gone. Are you going to tell me where she is?"

"Even if I knew, I wouldn't tell you. If she wanted to see you, she wouldn't have left without saying goodbye."

This wasn't happening all over again. He raked his hands through his hair and the sense of déjà-vu only grew stronger.

Rebekah set her hands on her hips. "She's my friend more than my employee, and I'm really mad at you for making her leave."

"I did not make her leave! I've been trying to persuade her to stay since the day we first met and I'm getting really tired of chasing after someone who doesn't want to be caught."

"Have you ever wondered why she doesn't want to be caught?"

"Of course I bloody have." He sank down into the nearest chair.

It happened to be by the window where he was in full public view, but he couldn't give a toss who spotted him right now. His heart had been torn out with a spoon and he had no energy left to spare on worrying whether his unshaved face would make tomorrow's papers. "I know she's scared of losing someone else she loves, but I have no idea how to convince her I'm not going to leave her."

"You can't. There are no guarantees in life." Rebekah slid into the chair across the table. "Just as you can't hold her here against her will."

He nodded. Of course he didn't want to trap Phoenix here. He wanted her happiness more than his own. But he still couldn't believe she was happier without him.

"She told me once that in me she'd found something to run *to*." He rubbed his hands over his face. That night in Vegas seemed a lifetime ago. He'd been hanging on to his memories, but perhaps it was time to accept that for Phoenix that night had never existed.

Rebekah rose, pausing midway as a thought struck her. "Have you told her you love her?"

He stared.

"Well?"

Had he? He couldn't honestly remember. He shrugged. It could hardly be that simple. "She knows."

Rebekah sighed. "Men!" Then her expression softened. "She said she wanted to go north for a while."

"If she sees the northern lights without me, I'm going to kill her." If he ever saw her again.

Once before, she'd disappeared off the face of the earth. She could do it again. And this time he had no faith in Destiny bringing her back to him. Destiny was a load of crock. If it were real, then Phoenix would have fallen as head over heels in love with him as he had with her and she wouldn't keep running away.

No, he had to face facts: her re-appearance in his life had been nothing more than coincidence, the legend of the sorceress was just another fairy tale and his wife didn't love him.

"I'm done chasing after her."

Rebekah's expression shut down. "Then if you don't mind, I have a café to open and you're scaring away my customers."

He glanced up through the window at the two middle-aged women hovering uncertainly outside the front door.

"Thanks for the talk, Bekah."

"Any time." But she'd already turned her back on him.

Phoenix settled into the chair at the one and only empty table at the busy waterfront café, ordered a chai latte and opened her book. Here she was, in an exotic European city of canals, great artworks and historic buildings, and all she could do was read?

But somehow having something to do helped her forget she was alone again. That there was no-one to stroll hand-in-hand with along the canal, or take a boat trip with, or discuss books or ideas with, or laugh with. Or make love to.

"Do you speak English?" At the sound of the very proper public school English accent, she looked up, into a pair of lively grey eyes below russet brown hair. "May I have a seat? Every other table is already full." He waved around the café. He didn't seem like a serial killer. In fact, he was quite attractive in a preppy sort of way. She nodded. "Feel free."

"Oh, you're American."

She nodded again and returned to her novel.

He didn't take the hint. "*The Rum Diary*. Have you seen the movie?"

She sighed and opened her mouth to tell him she didn't want to see the movie, she wanted to read the book. In peace. But an image flashed in her head, stopping her in mid breath.

She and Max had talked about books. She'd told him she hated

157

seeing the movie before reading the book. But it had been *Fear and Loathing in Las Vegas* they'd talked about. She frowned. She couldn't ever remember talking to Max about that book. Unless…

"So are you travelling alone?"

She closed the book and picked up her purse. "The table's all yours."

"I'm sorry. I didn't mean to disturb you. I saw a beautiful woman sitting alone and instinct kicked in." He smiled and there was a lot of charm in that smile. In another lifetime she might have looked twice after a smile like that. Now she wondered if she'd ever want to look twice again. There was only one man able to make her pulse race.

She stood. "You seem like a nice guy but I'm not interested. I'm not available."

He looked genuinely crestfallen. "You're not wearing a ring," he pointed out.

She looked at her left hand, as if seeing it for the first time. "You're right. I'm not."

She strolled away, down the edge of the canal, the book tucked under her arm and her thoughts a million miles away.

She and Khara had been on the night shift. They'd emerged from the casino's staff entrance shortly after dawn, blinking in the dazzling light of a new day, still too wide awake and hyped to go home and sleep. So they'd gone for a drink.

She was used to guys hitting on her and she was used to scoring free drinks. So when Max had bought her a drink, she'd figured 'Why not?'

The attraction had been instantaneous and mutual. Then he'd challenged her to a game of pool. She was really good at pool and he'd let her win that first game. The second had been more closely fought. The third … well, by then he'd won not just the game but her 'yes' to breakfast.

He'd just flown in from Europe and his body clock was even more messed up than hers. They'd settled on pancakes…

Phoenix screwed her eyes tight shut, blocking out the reflections of sunlight on water, and the noise of the tour boats plying the canal with speakers blaring.

After breakfast they'd walked. It didn't really matter where they went, only that they were together. Max held her hand and they talked about books and movies, about their dreams, about their families. They wandered into shops and laughed over kitsch tourist souvenirs and let a Japanese couple take their picture with Elvis in Madame Tussauds.

They shared a late lunch, not in a fancy restaurant but in a diner she knew that served good, homely food. He told her about his father's funeral. About how he finally felt free to follow his own path.

She'd told him about the long weeks nursing her Dad through chemo. How his death had set her adrift, as if the anchor holding her together had been lost.

The freedom he craved was the same freedom that had sent her running. She hadn't realised she'd been running *to* something rather than away until she met Max.

She'd been running towards a new life, a new destiny.

They'd shared a bottle of wine and talked until the diner closed, and then they'd stood on the sidewalk, in the dazzling light of the neon signs of The Strip and another fiery Vegas sunset, and shared their first kiss.

They stood, arms wrapped around each other, his hands tucked into the back pockets of her jeans to pull her close against him, and he said: "I won't mind if you think I'm completely out of my mind, because I probably am, but I'm in love with you."

Love. He'd used the L word within hours of knowing her. Not Lust, but Love. And the most insane part of it was, she'd felt it too.

159

He hadn't suggested they marry. *She* had.

Standing on a street corner, with traffic blaring past and the thump of music beating up through the soles of their feet. *I don't ever want this day to end. I want to spend the rest of my life with you. Isn't that crazy?*

He took both of her hands in his and the shining look he turned on her, burning brighter than any neon sign, anchored her. She clung to it, feeling safe and rooted for the first time in her entire life.

"Yes, it's crazy." His voice was soft and intense. "But this is the city of crazy. Let's do it." Right there on the sidewalk he got down on one knee. "Georgiana Phoenix Montgomery, will you marry me?"

"I can't."

He looked as though she'd hit him with a sledgehammer.

"I've done some stupid things in my life. I was caught with cannabis once and I have a criminal record. What would it do to your family, and your country, if that ever got out?"

He took both her hands in his. "I love that you make no apologies for who you are. It doesn't matter to me what anyone else thinks, as long as you and I have no secrets. And if it ever gets out, then we'll face it together."

She had to blink away the tears. For a moment, she hadn't even known what the burning sensation in her eyes was. She raised a hand to her cheek to catch the droplets.

Max looked aghast. "I'm sorry. I'm rushing this."

She shook her head. "I haven't cried since I was ten years old." She wiped away the tears, tears of joy rather than sadness. "We can't get married just like that, though. We need a license."

"Then tomorrow."

"If we're going to be crazy, why stop now? Khara's lived here her whole life, perhaps she'll know how to get a license."

While Khara's brother sorted the legal stuff, Khara insisted on an instant make-over. "You can't get married in jeans!" she'd said, aghast when Phoenix asked "Why not?"

Since they were both too broke to go shopping, Khara loaned her a dress, a knee-length halter neck dress in soft ivory. And shoes with actual heels. She probably looked like Marilyn Monroe but she didn't care. The look in Max's eyes as she walked down the aisle alone was worth all the effort.

There were no flowers, no cake, no rings, other than his old signet ring. Only simple vows spoken in low voices, that turned her into a princess. And she felt like a princess.

They kissed, and Khara cried, and then they'd opened the champagne, and the chapel's pianist had sprayed them with a glitter gun.

"The closest thing we'll get to a 21 gun salute," Max whispered, laughing as he bent to kiss her again.

Then they'd said goodbye to Khara and her brother, and Max took her back to his hotel room. The first time they'd made love, slowly exploring one another, she'd already had his ring on her finger.

Phoenix blinked. She remembered *everything*. Including that horrible morning after and not even knowing who Max was. Tears stung her eyes and this time she let them fall. The relief was overwhelming.

He'd known the worst there was to know about her and he'd still wanted her.

How could she not have known him? How could she have hurt him like that? And she'd kept on hurting him, digging the knife in deeper, pushing him away every time he got too close.

The real reason she'd pushed him away was because she'd been scared. Not of being trapped, or of losing her freedom. She'd been terrified of remembering how much she needed him. Of loving him so much that she couldn't live without him.

And Max had understood. *Your courage is bigger than your fear*, he'd said.

She closed her eyes against the flood of emotion. This strange feeling overpowering her … this was how it felt to care, to care so deeply that you would do anything for the one you loved. Even take on any responsibility, any duty, just to be with them, to see them happy.

"Don't do it!"

She opened her eyes to see a little old lady hurrying towards her, pulling along a dog on a lead. "Whatever burdens you carry, you can't give up," the woman said, breathless.

Phoenix smiled, ecstatic. "You're right. I can't give up. I have to go back."

She turned away from the canal, leaving the bewildered woman open-mouthed.

She didn't know if she'd make it back to Waldburg in time for the coronation. She wouldn't blame Max if he never wanted to see her again after all the pain she'd put him through. But she had to try.

Chapter Twelve

Every bus, boat and car in Westerwald was headed into Waldburg but even so, she'd been hard pressed to find a seat. As the packed bus wound along the road that ran beside the Wester river all the way from the big city of Neustadt to the far older town of Waldburg, Phoenix couldn't help but share the excitement of the people around her.

She was grateful she'd taken the time to darken her hair and the sunglasses helped too, as no one recognised her. She had no clue how she'd answer the inevitable questions if they did.

Number one being why was she here on an over-crowded municipal bus and not getting glammed up for her front row seat in the cathedral.

On the plus side, if Max would give her the time of day, she'd have a lot to tell him. He need have no fear of a referendum. Her fellow bus passengers were all big fans, increasingly so as the beer flowed and the bus drew closer to the coronation.

She shielded her eyes against the sun's glare as she stepped down off the bus at the terminus. The main pedestrian boulevard which ran down through the sloping town to the river embankment had been decorated with acres of bunting in blue and white, the nation's colours, and the dragon and rose motif dominated. The town was dressed in its full festive finery, the sidewalks crammed with people, music playing from speakers in every street and fountains of wine everywhere she turned.

It took her the better part of an hour to get from the bus station up into the old part of town, since everyone and their mother was headed the same way.

In the town square the café was closed. Phoenix stood at the locked door and glanced at her watch. She needed a plan and she needed it fast.

Already the luxury sedans passed through the square, a slow, stately procession of VIPs headed to the medieval cathedral within the town's walls.

The cathedral. In less than half an hour that's where Max would be. And that's where she would go. It was too late for a seat inside the cathedral, but there was no way she was missing the biggest day of his life.

Max stood before the tall mirror and cast a critical eye over his costume. He hadn't played dress-up in years and the uniform, which the seamstress had still been working on at dawn, was definitely one of the most elaborate he'd ever worn.

The gold braid winked in the light, as he moved to slide the thin sword into the stiff leather scabbard at his waist. The only thing missing from this outrageous outfit was the white plumed hat that went with the army's full ceremonial dress. Though since he'd already done a few practise walks with the crown of his ancestors on his head, he knew that was no piece of cake either.

He looked almost as ridiculous as he felt. Phoenix would have gotten a kick out of this.

His gut twisted.

Better not to think of her.

Better not to think of anyone he'd ever cared about.

He squared his shoulders. Phoenix had it right. It was better not to care. Caring only opened you up to heartbreak.

No matter how much you loved someone, no matter how much faith you had in them, still they let you down. Still they left you alone.

His breath stuck in his throat. Today should have been celebrated among friends and family. Instead, his family were scattered to the four winds and the best friend he had in the world had run away again.

"You look mighty fine!"

He turned at the sound of the familiar voice, the lump in his throat dissolving. "Granddad! What are you doing here?"

"You didn't think we'd leave you to do this all alone, did you? Your mother insisted your Gran and I come in her place." His normally twinkling eyes were grave. "She wasn't sure what reception she would get and didn't think having the populace hurl rotten tomatoes at the procession would help you much."

Max managed a laugh. "Damn right, it wouldn't." He enveloped the old man in a bear hug. His grandfather was still spry for his age, though these days Max dwarfed him by at least a head. "You haven't heard from Rik, have you?"

"He's safe, he's okay, and he sends you his best wishes. He still needs some time to adjust to the change in circumstances."

"Him and me both," Max muttered. "This should have been his day."

His grandfather shrugged. "Maybe, maybe not. Destiny has a way of making sure everything works out for the best."

Max snorted. "Don't you start on all that Destiny crap too. I've had about as much of it as I can take."

"That doesn't sound like you." His grandfather gripped his forearms and looked into his eyes. "You haven't been sleeping. And you look unhappy. Where's your girl – the one you met in Vegas?"

Max shrugged out of his grip and turned back to the mirror, straightening his epaulettes. "She's gone."

"Ah."

Exactly. Max couldn't have said it better.

"She running scared by all this?" The old man asked.

"Terrified out of her wits, and not just by the whole royal thing. And there's nothing I can do about it but let her go."

His grandfather moved to stand between him and the mirror, ensuring he had Max's attention. "I don't know much about the European side of your family, but I'll tell you this. My family arrived in America with nothing. They crossed the country in a horse-drawn wagon and carved out a home in a hostile land. They braved the Wild West and drought and depression. You come from a long line of fighters, and it's not in you to give up. You want her? Then you damn well fight for her. You hear me?"

Max felt himself grin for the first time in days. "I hear you, Granddad." It was nice to have someone in his corner who cared more about him than about the state of the nation.

"Your grandmother's waiting for me at the car and the officials in charge of the procession were very insistent we leave on time, so I better hurry." He headed for the door. "You knock 'em dead, son."

"I will." Max shook his grandfather's hand and watched until the old man had disappeared from sight. Then he moved to the desk to fetch the notes for his speech. These were the carefully chosen words he'd laboured over with Phoenix. He glanced through them and something settled in his stomach. Not the weight he was growing used to, but a sense of calm. He left the notes on his desk and headed out towards the waiting state car.

Max hadn't expected such crowds. Of course, he'd known many of the town's citizens would turn out, since the weather was good, and he knew there were people who'd made the journey from around the duchy courtesy of the free bus service he'd insisted on. But the press of people lining every street was unexpected. The cheer that rose up as his open-topped car emerged from the castle precinct was deafening and it continued unabated as the procession inched its way through the old part of town. Flags waved, banners wishing him well in every language imaginable hung from the buildings and the roar of the national anthem blaring from speakers engulfed him. He waved and waved, smiling without the forced expression he'd worn all week.

He could do this. He could even do it alone, if he had to. But he'd really rather not. *Fight for what you want.*

Granddad's words echoed around him, in the roar of the crowd, in the peal of the church bells, in the sirens of the bikes escorting him through the old town walls and into the wider streets of the newer part of town, downhill towards the cathedral, its golden bell tower glinting in the sunlight.

Fight for what you want.

He wanted to be the best Archduke this country had ever seen. He wanted to bring this nation into the 21st century and watch it grow and flourish. But that didn't mean he couldn't have everything else his heart desired too.

Even if Destiny needed a kick in the ass for him to get it.

The car pulled up before the stairs to the cathedral. A uniformed attendant opened the car door and Max stepped out. On the top step he paused and turned to wave to the crowd gathered in the open plaza in front of the cathedral. The cheer, impossibly, grew louder.

He felt their expectation like a physical force in the air. And something more, a sudden certainty that out there in the crowd, was the other half of his soul.

"We need to move inside now," the officious attendant said.

Max shook his head. "Everyone inside can wait. This day is for the people." Not for him, not for his cabinet, or for the visiting royals and heads of state from around the world. Today was for the people of Westerwald, who had travelled from around the country and perhaps even farther, to be here today, when they could be watching on television in the comfort of their own homes.

He smiled at the barrage of cameras in the crowd, waved again and only then did he turn on his heel and step inside the nave.

It took a moment for his eyes to adjust to the darkened interior and for his heart to adjust its rapidly skipping beat.

Then he began the long walk down the aisle, through the patches of coloured light showering down from the tall stained glass windows above. He wasn't alone. He had an entire nation at his back, a family who loved him, far away as they were, and a woman out there waiting for him to claim her.

Phoenix had managed to find a vantage spot on the steps of a building of law offices edging the cathedral's plaza. She was very far back, so the guests disembarking from the procession of smart sedans were little more than indistinguishable ants. But at least she could see over the heads of most of the crowd and the massive screens set up on either side of the square showed a view of the red carpeted aisle inside the cathedral.

A rather large family had wedged themselves into the same front doorway. The law firm's doors were firmly shut, though from the sounds of partying above the staff were enjoying their vantage point.

Divorce lawyers, Phoenix noted wryly, checking out the brass plate above her head.

She looked over the family crammed in beside her and did a quick head count. Five children, varying in age from teens to a babe in arms. Wow. And they'd still managed to make space for her. They'd come prepared too, with picnic basket, camera and binoculars.

A cheer rose up through the crowd, spreading like a Mexican Wave at a soccer match. In the distance, yet another elegant black luxury car pulled up before the cathedral, this one with its top down. It was like a Bentley convention had hit town today.

A uniformed figure emerged from the vehicle and her heart knocked against her ribs. A fair head caught the sunlight as Max climbed the stairs and paused at the elaborate cast bronze doors of the cathedral.

The watching TV cameras zoomed in and Max's face appeared on the massive screens positioned on either side of the plaza. He waved and the crowd went wild, the cheers reaching a deafening crescendo.

A tug began low in Phoenix's stomach and she found herself unable to breathe. On the screens, Max grinned, the dimples appearing in his cheeks.

"He's so nice," the mother with the infant in her arms beside her yelled over the noise of the crowd.

Phoenix nodded. Nice didn't even begin to cover it.

Across the plaza, Max turned and disappeared into the cathedral and the noise abated. Phoenix knew enough of the coronation ceremony to know there'd be music playing in the cathedral right now but she was too far away from the speakers to hear a thing.

"So where are you from?" the woman asked. The infant in her arms wriggled, bored now that the excitement levels around her had dropped.

"America," Phoenix answered.

"That's a long way to come for the coronation."

Phoenix shook her head. "I was passing through and this seemed like fun."

"It is! We haven't had this much fun in years. The previous

coronation was down in Neustadt and I was too young to remember the last royal wedding."

"I hear that didn't end so well."

The other woman shifted the fractious infant to her other hip. "They seemed happy and really that's all that counts, isn't it? Who am I to judge? I wasn't exactly a saint when I married Markus and he was already divorced with kids." She nodded at the teenagers in animated conversation with their dad on the other side of the doorway. That explained the passel of children.

The woman shrugged. "We all have baggage and none of us are perfect."

Phoenix nodded.

The infant tried to grab at her hair, and the mother shifted her to her other hip. "Sheesh, but I swear you keep getting heavier," she said to her baby.

The child laughed.

Phoenix couldn't help but smile back at the cheeky face. "I'll hold her a while, if you want." Now why the hell had she offered that?

The woman's smile was worth it, though. "You don't mind? Just for a moment?"

"No problem." Phoenix hoped she sounded surer than she felt. But really it wasn't a problem. The child settled on her hip, not quite so bored now that she had a different grown up to investigate. She wove chubby fingers into Phoenix's hair and Phoenix smiled. "It must have been a big adjustment marrying a man with children." Almost as big an adjustment as marrying a man with an entire nation to care for.

The woman shrugged but her dark eyes shone. "It's all worth it when you find the one you want to be with for the rest of your life. Sometimes we have to take the duty along with the desire."

She caught her husband's eye and he smiled back at her.

Phoenix's heart constricted. That was how her parents used to look at each other. With stars in their eyes.

Had she ever looked at Max like that?

Yes, on their first night together in Vegas. The night of their first date, first kiss, first wedding. First time they'd made love. And boy was that a memory worth having!

So why had she been fighting it ever since? That day and night she'd spent with Max she'd felt as though anything was possible. Even a home and a family. Together, they could have taken on the world. And they'd planned to.

She sighed. Until she'd woken with no memory and all her old fears.

"So do you have a man waiting for you somewhere?" The woman asked.

Phoenix shook her head. "I did. A really incredible man. But I blew it." Twice.

"If it's meant to be, then Destiny will take care of it."

Phoenix rolled her eyes. "What is it with the people of Westerwald and their belief in destiny?" And their faith in Happy Ever Afters.

She'd never believed in the former and she'd given up on the latter. She wouldn't be at all surprised if Destiny gave her a great big kick in the ass for screwing this one up.

"Things always seem to work out for the best. Like with the Archduke." The woman leaned closer, dropping her voice. "I know I probably shouldn't say this but I'm so glad it's Maximilian taking over from his father rather than Prince Fredrik."

"Why's that?" Phoenix asked.

"Fredrik seems like a decent enough guy but he's so stiff and formal. We're an easy-going people and we've had enough of stiff and formal. We need a bit of fun and lightness. Fresh blood, so to speak." The woman's brow wrinkled. "Though of course it's the old blood, because that was what the fuss was all about, but you know what I mean."

Phoenix nodded.

"And maybe we'll have another royal wedding soon and we can forget all the unpleasantness of the past. I wonder if we'll see her? She must be inside there somewhere."

Fear froze Phoenix's heart. "Who?"

"The waitress Maximilian's been dating. But if you haven't been here long, maybe you haven't heard?"

"Princes don't marry waitresses."

The child in her arms laughed. She was getting heavier by the moment, but it was a pleasant kind of weight. A pleasant kind of responsibility.

"Why not? Legend has it that the story of Cinderella originated right here in Waldburg. Why shouldn't it happen again?"

Because … Phoenix paused. She'd had a hundred and one reasons why not when she'd fled from Waldburg. None of them really seemed to matter. They'd all been excuses, really, not reasons.

"Thanks for holding her." The mother reached out her hands for her daughter. With a toothless smile that wrenched Phoenix's already overworked heart, the baby looked up at her mother, arms outstretched.

"It was my pleasure. What's her name?"

"Georgiana." Misunderstanding the look on Phoenix's face, she added defensively, "It's a very popular name here in Westerwald. It was the name of a legendary sorceress who cast a magic spell on the royal family some three hundred years ago."

"I've heard the story," Phoenix said, her voice dry. Max had clearly left out some of the more interesting details.

The woman held out her hand. "I'm Katherine."

"Pleased to meet you." Phoenix smiled as she shook Katherine's hand. "You won't believe this, but my name's Georgiana too. I was

172

named after my grandmother."

The grandmother who'd kicked her mother out when she'd fallen pregnant out of wedlock. Her mother had always said Phoenix was the baby born out of the ashes of her old life.

She wiped away another tear. What was it with these tears? It was almost as if once they got started, they wouldn't stop.

They watched as the coronation ceremony played out on the big screens like a silent movie. Phoenix wondered how Max was feeling. He certainly didn't look like someone with the weight of the world on his shoulders. Nor did he look like a man grieving for his wayward wife. He looked … determined.

The impulsive young man she'd married in Vegas was gone. In his place stood a finer man. If she'd loved him in Vegas, it had nothing on this feeling swelling inside her now.

My husband. The words no longer sounded alien.

The archbishop placed the crown on Max's bowed head, and they all cheered their support, as Markus popped open a bottle of champagne.

"Would you like some?" He offered Phoenix a plastic picnic cup full of bubbling gold.

She laughed. "Why not?" She'd already done the worst she could do and married then lost the love of her life. What harm could a few sips of champagne do?

Max stepped out of the cathedral into the brilliant sunshine and looked out over the crowd, thousands of faces turned expectantly toward him. The gem-encrusted crown weighed heavy on his head and he had to lift his chin high to keep it balanced.

In the wake of the pealing cathedral bells, the hush that fell over the square was eerie. Even eerier was the incomprehensible feeling that Phoenix was out there in the crowd.

Smiling for the cameras, he drew in a deep breath and stepped

173

up to the microphone placed ready on the broad top step.

"I think it's fair to say that none of us ever expected it to be me standing here in front of you today. Least of all me." The crowd tittered, a little embarrassed. "I was raised on the idea that a certain destiny awaited me. If there's anything I've learned these past few months it's that nothing is certain, not even destiny. But these last few months have also taught me the importance of faith."

"In this magnificent setting we are reminded of the traditions of our past. But today isn't about looking back. It's about looking forward. For too many centuries, we in Westerwald have lived in fear, afraid of a return to civil war and anarchy, afraid of rocking the boat. And as a result, we've gone from a once mighty nation to a little country hardly known beyond our own borders. We are a nation that rewards mediocrity and those who want greatness leave our country to seek their fortunes elsewhere."

He paused. The crowd's attention was riveted on him but he felt their uncertainty as they wondered where he was going with this. He lifted his chin.

"It is time for us to let go of our past fears and to move forward. I have faith in our future. I believe Westerwald will again be a great nation, a leader among nations, a country to be proud to claim as ours.

"Inside this cathedral today I made the same vows that my ancestors have made to the government of Westerwald for generations. But now I want to make another vow, a vow between me and you, the people of this nation: I vow to do everything in my power to make this country great again."

He had them now. At his rousing call, their support rolled over him in a wave. He waited for the cheers to subside. "But I cannot do this alone. I need you with me." He prayed that his words were reaching the one pair of ears that most needed to hear them.

"What makes a nation truly great is not its economic wealth, or

174

its power over other nations, or its military force, but its people. It is our unity and our diversity that makes us strong. Together, we can achieve anything."

The crowd roared its approval, the cheers and applause bouncing off the walls that surrounded the plaza. He waited until the clamour had dropped enough that he could be sure his next words would be heard. "I cannot do this alone. I need a partner at my side who will support me, love me and have faith in me. Phoenix, if you're out there, I want you to know that person is you. I love you and I need you here with me."

The buzz began as a low sound, rising as people twisted to search in their midst for her. Max held up his hands, demanding the quiet he needed for his final words. "Georgiana Phoenix Montgomery, will you marry me?"

He wasn't seriously doing this! This wasn't the speech they'd laboured over together. This was…insane.

Phoenix's tears flowed freely now, running down her cheeks in hot rivulets that she had no control over. Katherine looked at her oddly.

"Champagne always does this to me," Phoenix muttered, wiping her eyes.

"It's you, isn't it?"

Oh God, no. Not here. Not with all these people watching. She opened her mouth to deny it, but Katherine took the plastic cup from her hand and nudged her. "You have to go to him."

Phoenix's eyes widened as she looked out over the sea of people. "Don't be crazy. How am I going to get through that crowd?"

The teenage daughter handed her a tissue and she blotted her face.

"The old fashioned way," Markus said, grinning. He placed his fingers in his mouth and whistled. "Future princess coming through," he shouted.

The people in front of them turned to look. Phoenix shrunk back but Markus took her arm and led her forward. "You heard the man. Together, we can do anything. Let's go."

This was insane. It must be the champagne. She was going to wake up tomorrow with a mighty headache to find this was all a dream. Or a nightmare, she couldn't quite decide which way this was headed yet.

Markus was tall and broad-shouldered and he ploughed into the crowd, carving a path for Phoenix. Katherine squeezed her hand, then Phoenix followed, holding her head high and hoping the tears hadn't left marks on her face or run her mascara. She'd never tested the waterproof claims of her make-up before.

As the word spread through the crowd, people moved aside, clearing a path right across the plaza, straight to the steps leading up to the cathedral doors.

In the periphery of her vision, Phoenix saw the view on the massive screens at the front of the crowd shift to take in the plaza, zooming in on the shifting crowd, searching for her.

She couldn't bear to look.

She followed Markus, staying close, trying hard to keep a smile in place and her head high under the thousands of curious gazes. Her cheeks ached from the effort.

They reached the bottom of the great stone steps. Her blood pounded. She struggled to breath.

Then Markus stepped aside and she looked up, straight into a pair of cool, amused, blue eyes. Something shifted inside her. The panic and fear were gone. A warm, delicious calm filled her.

Their audience melted away as she climbed the stairs towards him. The crowd was insignificant. Only one thing mattered, and that was the man standing before her with stars in his eyes.

"You idiot," she said, keeping her voice low and just for him.

"You know we're already married."

"It seems like I have to keep reminding you. So what do you say?" He held out his hand. She felt rather than heard as the crowd at her back held its breath.

"Do you promise we'll still get to travel and see the world?"

"Of course."

"And we don't have to start a family right away?"

"Not until we're ready."

"And no-one's going to tell me how to dress or what to do?"

He frowned. "Enough already. Do I have to remind you that I don't believe in divorce and bigamy is illegal in Westerwald, so you're going to have to go through with a big, white wedding in full view of the TV cameras whether you want to or not?"

She laughed and took his hand. "Well, when you put it like that…I do."

He wrapped his arm around her waist, pulled her hard against him, and tilted her chin for a kiss. The crowd erupted.

"Damn crown. I can't kiss you properly!" He pulled away.

"If I remember correctly, your schedule allows you a thirty minute break before the garden party. That should be more than enough time." She melted against him. "For more than just a kiss."

Epilogue

They stood on the stone ramparts of the castle, looking down over the town towards the river where brightly lit barges lay against the dark water. From their decks, fireworks shot up, a kaleidoscope of colour and patterns bursting into the sky.

Max squeezed Phoenix's hand. That half hour in his suite hadn't been enough but now the garden cocktail party was over, the gala dinner was over and they were alone at last.

He trailed the fingers of his free hand down the soft curve of her cheek and she turned her face into his palm.

"I love you," he whispered, his heart pulling tight at the words. He really hadn't told her enough. He planned to tell her every day for the rest of their lives.

She lifted her dark, burning gaze to his. "I love you too."

She let go his hand and reached up to unclasp the chain from around her neck. "The first time you gave me this you told me it was a sign that I was no longer alone. That I had a family to belong to and a home."

His eyes widened in shock. "You remember?"

She nodded, eyes bright with tears. "I remember everything." She wiped her eyes. "And I seem to have turned into a waterworks too."

She slipped the ring off the chain and held it out to him. He took it with fingers that shook almost as much as they'd done the first time he'd done this. Then he slid the ring onto her finger. Not the ring finger of her left hand, but her right hand. "It's an old Westerwald custom that during the engagement the bride wears the ring on her right hand. When we marry publicly, I'll move it to your left hand."

He folded her fingers in his and she smiled, the private, sexy smile she kept just for him.

"There's only one thing I don't remember. I still have no idea why you married me."

"Then let me remind you." He cupped her face with his hands and leaned close to kiss her and the fireworks above them were nothing on the fireworks inside.

CPSIA information can be obtained
at www.ICGtesting.com
Printed in the USA
LVHW111227180520
655873LV00001B/7